Ogden's Story

by

Dan Turpen

I am always at a loss to know how much to believe of my own stories.

Washington Irving
Tales of a Traveller, To The Reader

Acknowledgements

Thanks to James Ian Mair for the cover photograph and illustration. Thanks to James Stevenson and Jeffrey W. Johnson for assistance with technical matters. Thanks to Joyce A. Turpen, Clinton August Turpen and James M. Mair for reading the manuscript and providing insight and suggested clarification. Thanks to those who contributed in ways I cannot attribute as their experiences, observations, expressions and truths have taken on a different reality and application as the writer wove them into the story. D.T.

PREFACE

As he stood inside the gate of their small vegetable garden and surveyed sagging and rotted remains of plants gone to waste for want of water throughout a scorching, endless summer, Daniel Raithone Tyler turned and stepped back through the gate and hooked the latch. Disgusted by the carnage he had witnessed, he walked a few steps and sat down on the shed porch. As he looked back at the garden, he recalled the promise once-flourishing plants had offered when spring rain and warm sunshine had worked their botanical miracle and how the now-withered husks had taken root and proclaimed their potential bounty. Unrealized potential and unfulfilled promise, Daniel once again reminded himself, had become the summary of his life in more ways than he cared to enumerate. Such thinking heaped more anguish onto a weakened vessel struggling to stay afloat but did not give him cause to recognize or accept only he was responsible for the way his life had unfolded.

How many years, he thought as he continued to feed his surging internal rant, have I struggled with this brick-hard damned clay? How many bales of peat moss and how many tons of compost and sand have I hauled and mixed into this unyielding bastard? How many hours have I wasted, he welcomed the heated momentum of his frustration and anger as they began to build, plowing, tilling, weeding and sweating my ass off and for what?

The failure to grow vegetables wasn't the true source of his discontent. The source of his aggravation was all about the failure of having something turn out as he had anticipated. It was all about having something to show that, damn it all, he could succeed at something. By his warped reasoning, failure at gardening and failure concerning other matters far beyond his control easily became personal affronts that he allowed to gnaw at his mind.

Once about every ten years, it seemed to him, sufficient and regular rain would fall and keep the clay soil loose enough to allow plants to mature and the harvest become worth his effort. This had not been one of those years and he now vowed that next spring he would not be out tilling and working on a futile project. If his wife, Lucy, had a contrary plan, she could do the work herself or hire someone to help her. A failed garden, along with so many other disappointing aspects of his life, had left him tired of fighting losing battles.

As far back as he could remember Daniel often felt constrained and unable to break free of binding chords that held him prisoner and brought a physical restlessness he was either unable or unwilling to confront or to explain to his wife and children. During those interludes when he was able to suppress his anxiety, whether for a few weeks or, on occasion, several months, he was productive and relatively happy. His wife and children could never anticipate or understand his sudden change of mood from one extreme to the other. He never mentioned or made excuses concerning his troubling feelings of hopelessness that altered his behavior and stifled his interaction and ability to love the people who loved him. After the children moved away to attend school and lead their own lives, Lucy often sensed she was at odds with a stranger whose dark moods were becoming deeper and longer in duration.

Without benefit of professional intervention, Daniel diagnosed the source of his anguish and misery. He was convinced his sense of imprisonment originated during his early infancy. The memory was real enough to him that when he recalled or imagined how he had felt during those episodes, he would become nervous and physically agitated. Although his claim, he admitted, contradicted psychologists who held such early memories to be far outside the bounds considered normal and therefore measurable, the science did give credence to the effects of early-life mental imprinting. Even if he could not prove what he vividly remembered, he knew the experience had seeded his being from which a life of discontent had grown.

He was convinced that sometime during his early months of life, he had been clad in full-length pajamas that covered his body from his neck to his toes. The garment that encased him so tightly eventually caused him to become too warm. Try as he might by twisting, turning, squirming and crying, as he believed had occurred, he could not break free of the binding bondage whose purpose and usage was to keep him warm and comfortable. He felt helpless and his frustration, it seemed, generated an anger that he did not understand or able to effectively direct. The source of his early unhappiness, he believed, was a loving parent who wanted to protect her child, not make his early life miserable. Why hadn't his vivid imprint, his memory, been that of a loving, maternal act? Why had his feeling of confinement, of struggle and discontent, been the memory that had misguided him and left him feeling unable to experience life as a man free to love and accept love?

That early tormenting experience, he thought, had been a precursor to a life of barriers he had not been strong enough to overcome. Now, years after he first relived his struggle with unseen, undetectable constraints, he still fought with forces he could not identify or understand. An unshakable feeling of restraint and struggle kept him focused on his failures rather than able to accept and celebrate his triumphs.

As he stood and walked away from the shed porch and headed toward the house, after yet another survey of his shortcomings and resultant disappointments, he could not have imagined what the oncoming months of his life would present.

CHAPTER 1

Daniel's first day on the job as a representative for a Bloomington, Indiana insurance agency also marked the day he met Ogden Royal. His first day as an agent, he learned later, marked Ogden's tenth year within those same walls. Ogden was an old-timer, in parlance and culture of that business. Agents who stayed around, successfully meeting their production goals, for more than one or two years were a rarity. Ogden, based on his longevity, was a person newly hired personnel respected and hoped to emulate. While that job, one of many he would quit, became an insignificant experience and easily forgotten, he would never forget Ogden Royal.

His first reaction toward Ogden was one of suspicion and an unexplainable dislike. Ogden projected a discernable air of aloofness and tended to remain by himself. The man just did not square with Daniel's mental image of someone with whom he could, or should, establish anything more than a working relationship held at arm's length. If his first impression proved credible, Ogden and he would pass in the hallway and go about their business with minimal interaction. To complicate his sense of discomfort concerning his new acquaintance, his office was located across the hall from Ogden. When they left their doors open, which was often, they could overhear one another as they conducted business by telephone. As days culminated into weeks, he would have cause to re-visit his early, pre-mature and erroneous appraisal of Ogden Royal.

His new acquaintance, as Daniel would realize, was not remote or an unfriendly person. Though he was quiet in manner, he was not lacking self-confidence. Ogden, small in stature, obviously enjoyed benefits derived from physical fitness. While not grotesquely muscled, his thick, trim torso bespoke of a time when he had likely relied upon his physical strength and endurance as he now did mental prowess. When Ogden arose to walk around his desk when the agency manager brought Daniel by his office for an introduction, though agile, Daniel noticed he displayed a pronounced limp that favored his left leg. Ogden did not refer to his physical impairment and other employees never mentioned his obvious handicap. It would be much later in their relationship before Ogden would become motivated and willing to discuss that subject.

Ogden knew the insurance business and knew how to deal with people. He was successful because he was honest, forthright and knowledgeable. Clients came to him with their problems and Ogden would help them chart the best course of action. Daniel soon realized that if you didn't want an honest answer, you should not pose him a question or share a concern. "If you sought re-assurance for a wrong-headed plan," Daniel related to his wife Lucy, "he wasn't the person to further your error by his agreement or silence." When clients visited Ogden to complain of an increased auto insurance premium, he never hesitated to remind them they had "earned" the increase by their careless driving habits.

During the few years Daniel worked with Ogden, he could not recount a client speaking disrespectfully or displaying irritation toward Ogden personally. "The truth, from him," Daniel said, "freed clients from anger and their feeling of unfair treatment by the company." Ogden wasn't "acting" out of a pseudo-sense of superiority. Ogden wasn't acting at all. He had earned his respected status in the hierarchy of that agency and within the insurance industry based on his character and reliability.

Other employees frequently consulted Ogden with a variety of concerns. He seemed to be the office sounding board for agents, the manager and clerical personnel. Ogden, Daniel came to learn and appreciate, provided sound guidance when consulted. As his initial evaluation began to change, he would interrupt his neighbor across the hall when he wasn't sure how to handle a situation. Ogden was the resident geographic wizard when other agents needed help in finding a particular location when the company home office ordered pictures of insured buildings or an appointment was off the usual, well-known roads and lanes. This was several years before GPS technology and county maps were not always reliable.

Daniel's relationship with his neighbor slowly developed as Ogden assumed the role of a patient and reliable teacher. "Ogden, during the few years we worked together, certainly didn't need or gain much from me," Daniel told Lucy. "It was I, the rooky agent, who was the needy part of that relationship."

It was just a matter of days before his judgmental, negative appraisal of Ogden became a faint memory. Many years afterward, Daniel had occasion to recall, "I can't believe how wrong I had been about another person. As I look back, I consider Ogden Royal the only lasting friendship I ever made or maintained."

Although he had become more comfortable with their working relationship, Daniel continued to address Ogden as "Mr. Royal." Ogden volunteered he should dispense with that formality and address him by his first name. "Unless, of course, you insist that I address you as 'Mr. Tyler,'" he added without any hint of levity.

Not long after that easing of their interaction, Daniel began calling Ogden Royal, "O.R." "He didn't object or comment on that shortened, more familiar version of his name but none of the other office personnel were adventurous enough to cross that line themselves," Daniel remembered.

The story Ogden would share with Daniel took place several years after their common employment and working relationship ended. Daniel, like most agents, left the agency after about two years. Ogden continued to work there for another five years, or so, before he took a new position. Over the years apart, they had not maintained regular contact and often a year or two would pass before they crossed paths. When they did meet, it was for a quick cup of coffee and, on rare occasions, for their version of golf. Ogden and Daniel liked to be outdoors; golf had once served as a convenient medium. "We improved our golf scores by allowing mutually agreed upon mulligans in order to keep our game within a few hours instead of, perhaps, all day," Daniel recalled years later when he thought of those occasions when two duffers enjoyed being together.

Ogden's lameness didn't hamper his play and he was far better at their diversion than his younger partner. "We would hash over local current events and interests as we made our way around the course," Daniel stated his recollection to Lucy. "Ogden, without children of his own, always asked about my three children and what they were doing. We would go our separate ways with the agreement to meet again at a non-committal, 'sometime.'" Up until the time this story begins, that "sometime" turned out to be over four years.

Early in August 2008, after Ogden had retired and Daniel was pursuing other avenues of gainful employment, he left several messages on Ogden's home answering machine suggesting they might meet for a round of golf or for a less time-consuming cup of coffee. Daniel hadn't called Ogden because he wanted anything from his old friend, but rather to re-establish contact with a man he admired and held in high esteem. Unlike the usually responsive Ogden, those calls went un-answered. After a few stabs at making contact, Daniel decided to stop calling. He had assumed Ogden was occupied with other matters or simply wasn't interested in re-kindling a friendship that had abated due to mutual inattention. It would be almost two months before Daniel heard from O.R.

When Ogden called in mid-October, Daniel noticed his tone was brusque and his voice seemed strained and weak as he began, "Ogden here. How about meeting tomorrow for a few minutes and we'll have a cup of coffee?"

"While not unlike him to come straight to the point, I detected Ogden wasn't his usual positive self, and he didn't sound particularly pleased to be speaking with me," Daniel recalled. "I suspected his slow response to my earlier contacts was from a sense of obligation he might have felt toward an old acquaintance. If that turned out to be the case, I would meet with him this time but I wouldn't bother him again. After all, why struggle to keep a friendship viable if one party feels pressed to do so? Whatever his reason for finally returning my calls, I looked forward to seeing and talking with him. I could never have imagined what had prompted Ogden to meet with me," Daniel remembered.

"O.R., what a surprise! It's good to hear from you," he replied while assessing the strained voice he detected. "You name the place and time and I'll be there. Sounds like you have a cold. Are you doing okay?"

"Sure," was the faint answer, "must be a bad connection or maybe I'm too far from a tower. Say about 10 tomorrow morning there at Smitty's?"

"Okay, that's fine with me. I'll plan to see you at Smitty's. I'm looking forward to talking with you, Ogden, and…" Without waiting for him to complete his thought, the caller ended the brief conversation.

With a brief note in his journal, Daniel wrote he was relieved to have finally heard from Ogden, but his matter-of-fact, almost business-like demeanor and that thin, strained vocal intonation had stuck in his mind. "Perhaps," he consoled himself, "as Ogden had volunteered, it was just a matter of poor telephone service."

When they met the following morning, Ogden looked older and thinner than Daniel remembered or expected. As a former Army Ranger, Ogden had always prided himself in his bearing, neat attire and healthful habits. Ogden didn't seem to be the person, from his appearance, whom Daniel had envisioned he would be meeting.

"O.R., it's good to see you. How have you been? It's been a long time since we last met!" Daniel began as they walked slowly toward the side door at Smitty's diner on a brisk, sunny October morning.

"Ah, good enough for an old codger, I suppose. Let's go inside, get a cup of coffee and talk for awhile," Ogden replied without enthusiasm or hint of a smile to Daniel's greeting. Upon that terse response, they entered the restaurant, went to the counter and ordered coffee. Ogden then chose a booth near the door they had entered and out of earshot of other patrons.

"So, are you still writing these days?" Ogden began as he began to stir his coffee and seemed to struggle at situating himself in a comfortable sitting position.

"Well, no, at least not for the local paper. They seem to entertain a certain perspective I don't satisfy. What I wrote must have ruffled the feathers of those who don't want to read or hear how this country has remained strong throughout our comparative brief history. I suppose I wasn't radical enough, not a rabid liberal seeking to rip-up the social and political fabric that I believe holds us together."

"I can understand that. Somehow, you never struck me as one holding tight to either side of the political curve. This community is unlike anywhere in Indiana due to the influence of the university. The fact that you were able to write for as long as you did is to your credit. You must have had a good readership or they would have shucked you right from the start," Ogden surmised, as he seemed to be more at ease.

"I tried to understand issues from as many views as possible but I always took a stance. Whatever position I took, I didn't leave much doubt in the minds of readers. If I had been a waver of a radical flag, I would probably still be writing for the paper. I wasn't willing to abandon what I believe and the editor wasn't willing to allow me to continue.

"Anyway, I did self-publish a short book and I write two blogs and participate in several on-line forums that keep me busy. A weekly paper contacted me and indicated interest in running my column, but they aren't anxious to pay very much for the material. You know, people don't seem to see much value in anything they can't eat, drink, drive or wear."

"Well, to hell with doing anything for free that puts more money into greedy pockets," Ogden replied. "After all," he continued, "if it's worth writing and interesting enough that someone wants to include in something they sell, its worth something to the person who wrote it."

"I suppose they figure writing doesn't cost much, just paper and ink, so the material should be given away. I don't know how editors think, but I do know writing is one damn rough way to earn a dollar," Daniel chuckled as he added liquid creamer to his coffee.

"I don't know much about writing or publishing, but it sounds pretty much like everything else. Too many people seem to want something but they don't want to pay for it."

With that terse observation, O.R. became quiet and returned to stirring at his coffee while Daniel awaited his next statement or question that might spur further conversation and break what was becoming an uncomfortable encounter.

"Did you play much golf this summer?" Daniel finally ventured to break the prolonged silence that had become burdensome, while hoping to prompt a reply that might explain those unanswered telephone messages.

"I haven't been on a golf course for over four years. Guess I've lost interest. I have too many other things going on for me to think about golf. How about you, have you been playing?"

"You know I was never much of golfer, O.R," Daniel answered. "I haven't played since we were out, how long has it been, four or five years ago? Like you, whenever I have time for golf, I always seem to find something else to do."

"Dan", Ogden began, "my wife told me you had called and left messages for me a few times here lately. I meant to get back with you but I've been a little under the weather. I've been in the hospital several times since the last time we visited. I've been in and out of more clinics and hospitals from here to Indianapolis than what I can remember. Nothing has been too effective so far, but who knows? Jane and I keep hoping one chemical or the other will get the job done and buy me more time."

"What…more time…what's the matter…why didn't you let me know, Ogden? At least I could have stopped by to see you. What's been going on with you? Hospitalized? Ogden, I had no way of knowing…" Daniel stammered, suddenly overcome by guilt generated by his initial thoughts that Ogden had been too busy or uninterested to maintain their relationship.

Ogden again became quiet and fixed his gaze on the door behind where they were sitting. He was obviously guarding against any chance their eyes would meet as he decided how he would say what was on his mind and instantly take this meeting in a direction far different from what Daniel had anticipated. After a silence that seemed like minutes, he lowered his gaze and began to speak.

"I've been diagnosed with incurable cancer that began in my prostate. From there, it has kept spreading. Knock it out one place and it appears somewhere else. I know I'm a goner and that's one reason I wanted to see you this morning."

"Ogden, how can I help you? Whatever I can do for you, just say the word." Daniel struggled to continue as his voice began to break, "I don't know what to say, except all those things people usually come up with when they hear bad news from a friend. I'm shocked to hear about your illness, of course. You have been a friend since we met back in 1978. I had begun to suspect something wasn't quite right with you, but had no way of knowing…"

"A person can only play mental gymnastics concerning what they'll do or feel if they learn they are dying," he interrupted when he sensed Daniel was stammering toward an unnecessary commiseration. "I know, for me at least, I was unprepared. I went through a phase where I wanted to believe all this might go away if I didn't give in and acknowledge it. Well, that does not work. Here lately, I've been facing the truth and that's why I wanted to see you this morning. You are right, Dan. Up until now, you had no way of knowing what was going on with me."

"I admit I was concerned, O.R., but I didn't want to become a nuisance or pry into something that wasn't any of my business or might offend you. I had convinced myself you were just busy and didn't want to be bothered with the likes of me. I hope and pray for your recovery. You know that, don't you?" With that, Daniel slumped back in the booth attempting to digest what had been a startling revelation.

Again, Ogden paused before he responded to that pained-ridden reply. Daniel remembered, "I tried to disguise the sorrow and fear I was feeling for my old friend, but Ogden, adept at reading body language and vocal tone, readily sensed my concern and shocked reaction to his acknowledgement and apparent acceptance of looming death."

Ogden continued, "What I'm going to ask you, you'll want to think about before you answer. You may not want to agree to anything I'm going to ask of you and that will be alright. I don't want to involve you if you aren't certain you want the responsibility. What I'm about to ask you must remain between the two of us. There will come a time, when what I tell you won't matter to me, *but it does now!* After that, what I will tell only you, worthwhile or worthless, will be your property. At that time, you will be free to use that property however you see fit."

"What you'll tell…me…?"

Ogden paused to take a sip of coffee, and between labored breaths, managed to continue, "Yes. Let me finish. In short, Doctor Dan, what I tell you, you must hold as a strict secret. How long will secrecy be necessary? I can't determine that today because I don't know today. Do you want me to continue?"

"Dr. Dan," brought Daniel back to a happier time when O.R. had hung that pseudo-title on him about the time he began calling Ogden by his initials. The "D" and the "R" were initials of Daniel's first and middle names. That's how Daniel had earned the title of "Doctor" from O.R. Daniel gained fleeting comfort from Ogden's reversion to a more playful time and a brief interjection of mirth from him. Perhaps whatever was to follow wasn't as murky and dire as he had begun to imagine.

"Now it was me that became mute and avoided eye contact as I considered what Ogden had told me, and growing apprehensive concerning what he might ask," Daniel wrote. "My mind whirled as I imagined what it was that he could possibly need me to do that demanded a pledge of secrecy."

"O.R., I'll do whatever I can for you as long as you aren't asking me to break the law," Daniel offered trying to continue in a more whimsical, playful mood. He knew whatever Ogden needed from him wasn't likely anything of that nature but he was attempting to lighten a conversation that had created such heavy suspense in his mind."

"Well, actually, Dan, my request of you is actually two favors. The first will begin upon your acceptance to do some writing for me. The second part, as I said, will take place at a future date. As I said before, I can't tell you when you will carry out my second request. Keep in mind, if you agree to help me, a large part of what I will tell you must remain private until I tell you differently. I know you to be honest; otherwise, I wouldn't be having this conversation with you. You tell me, when or even if I'm to continue."

"Ogden," Daniel replied, stalling to think, "let me go get us a re-fill. I'll be right back and we can continue our talk." With that lame excuse, Daniel stood and walked slowly to the counter as troubling thoughts of secrecy and mystery raced through his mind. What could Ogden Royal want him to write that required a vow of strict confidence?

CHAPTER 2

When he returned to their booth, Ogden was half-sitting, almost lying in his seat. Daniel remembered he couldn't help himself from comparing the thin, sick person now half-sitting, half-lying there to the robust, healthy person he had known throughout the past thirty or so years. Having witnessed his father go through the peaks and ultimate valley of terminal cancer, he recognized Ogden to be in a weakened state that blazoned an end that wasn't likely to be far in the future. Upon recalling an unmistakable sign his father had displayed, he studied Ogden's eyes.

He had never forgotten the terror he experienced when he happened to look across the table at his father as the family was enjoying a Sunday dinner. "I'll always remember when I first noticed my father's eyes had become rounded and sunken. I had come to believe, we all had believed, he was winning his battle with cancer. Then I knew. I didn't need a medical expert to provide a prognosis. His eyes, speaking loud and clear, told me more than what I wanted to acknowledge. Not long after the hollowness appeared, my father became helpless and died within a few weeks.

"I was somewhat comforted," Daniel summarized in his notes, "that Ogden's disease hadn't progressed to that extent." Prompted by the memory of his father, he relived emotions he hoped he would never experience again. Whatever Ogden needed from him, he thought, he would do his best to fulfill.

"I need to get back home," he volunteered in a barely audible voice when Daniel returned to their booth, "I'm not up to sitting on these hard seats for very long. As you have probably noticed, my get-up has got-up and gone!"

"Ogden," Daniel interjected, "I'll agree to your terms if you can accept one condition. If, for whatever reason, we reach a point where I think I can no longer be of help to you, I'll let you know. Anything you have shared with me, up to the point where I may beg off, will remain unspoken and you can have or destroy whatever notes or records I've taken up to that time. I'll do whatever I am able to do. I'll do my best to do what you need and want. Is this condition acceptable to you? If you can agree to that, I'll help you. Just say the word." If Ogden agreed to that, Daniel thought, he would have an established exit strategy if the need should arise.

Upon hearing Daniel's willingness to participate, Ogden mustered strength and managed an upright position. "Yes, that's fair. Okay, Dan, here is what I'm asking of you. First, I want you to write what I tell you. This will involve meeting with me, as I'm able, and recording what I need to say. In other words, I want you to be my biographer. Never thought I would ever say that to anyone," Ogden paused; either feigning a smile or winced, then continued, "I'm almost shocked to hear myself make such a request.

"As I said earlier, there are parts of what I'll tell you that must be held in strict confidence. What you write will become your property to keep and use how you may see fit, *but when that is to happen must remain my call*. I'll have that written up in legal terms so nobody can ever question my intent or your interests. After all, as we discussed earlier, the writer should benefit, in some way if the account is worthwhile, for what he writes. I have no problem with that. You will have earned the right, if you think appropriate, to benefit in some manner from what I'll tell you. Don't go into this thinking this will be easy or quick," Ogden continued, "because you will spend some time with me and, remember, there is a second part to our agreement."

"I still don't know why we have to be secretive, Ogden, if all you need is somebody to write for you," Daniel stated in hope the repeated stipulation calling for his pledge to keep the matter "just between the two of us" had been unnecessary.

"Listen to me carefully, there is a substantial part of what I intend to tell you that requires what I have asked. Please understand..." Ogden sounded irritated that Daniel seemed to be questioning his reasoning, "I wouldn't make such a request if I didn't believe it to be best...*for both of us*. Will you trust me that far? Will you record what I tell you and reserve judgment until you have more information? You'll see what I am asking of you is reasonable."

"Okay, O.R., whatever you need," Daniel replied noticing Ogden's discomfort and demonstrated need for a more comfortable accommodation. "I'll write for you and keep it to myself until you release me from my promise and grant your approval. When do we meet again to get started?"

"I'll call you in a few days," Ogden answered. "I'll contact my attorney, Tom Arthur, and have the agreement written, as I mentioned earlier. I'll have a copy of that document for you to read at our next meeting. After that initial reading, you'll need to go to the attorney's office to sign the document, ask any questions you have or to make changes. Anyway, I think you should meet Tom. He's a fine fellow that won't steer either of us wrong.

"By the way, would you be willing to come to my house the next time we meet? I think we would both be more comfortable there and certainly more private. Is that alright with you?"

"I don't have a problem coming to your home if that's what you want. Wherever you want to meet and talk will be fine with me," Daniel realized Ogden's need for secrecy whatever it entailed would remain unknown until their next meeting, if they would, in fact, ever meet again.

"O.R., call me when you want me to come to your place. I'll not bother you with telephoning. The ball is in your court," Daniel stated. "My schedule is flexible, so you can let me know when you want to meet again. I'll try my best to work on your schedule. By the way, do I tell my wife about your health condition? She'll be asking about you, so how do you want me to answer?"

Daniel recalled Ogden didn't hesitate at this query as he answered in a barely audible voice, "My health status is no great secret. I don't care, at this point, who knows what's going on with me. Anyway, you might use my illness as a plausible reason for your upcoming visits to my place. You know, giving comfort and diversion to an old friend. Does that excuse seem reasonable and believable?"

"Okay, O.R., as long it's alright that I tell Lucy what you told me about your condition. I'll wait to hear from you." With that, Daniel walked his old friend to his vehicle and watched as he drove slowly onto the highway and headed for his home. As he toyed with his keys and stood motionless on the sidewalk in front of his car, he thought about what he had just heard and observed and hoped Ogden would have a restful afternoon at home.

CHAPTER 3

Daniel drove the three miles to his home strictly by muscle memory, as he wasn't conscious of where he going or that he was driving. His thoughts swirled around what his old friend had told him, or rather not told him. What would he tell Lucy about his conversation with Ogden? Lucy knew they were meeting so she would have questions concerning why Ogden had been so slow in returning his calls. She would likely question why he would be going to Ogden's home for future meetings. Daniel decided he would not lie to her. He wouldn't break his promise to Ogden, of course, so he planned to have a sit-down discussion when he arrived home.

He decided he would ask Lucy for her understanding as he told her what Ogden had requested. "I'll tell her the truth, which is that I'll be helping him write whatever he wants written," Daniel thought. "At this time," as he further considered his pending explanation, "I can't say why Ogden wants this done and I don't know what he intends to have recorded. I'm in the dark on this matter up to that point. When I know more, and free to share more of whatever is to come, Lucy will be the first person I'll tell."

Ogden's statement concerning why he had insisted on Daniel's vow of secrecy re-played in his mind. What was he saying, Daniel mused, when he said, "I wouldn't make such a request if I didn't believe it to be best...*for both of us*"? Was Ogden indicating by including that addendum to his request that he might become involved in a matter he wouldn't be willing or prepared to undertake? "I'll decide that later," Daniel continued to cross-examine and console himself. "After all," he remembered, "I did gain his agreement that if my involvement became more than I was willing to undertake, I would let him know. The key to my future well-being," he studied, "may be not to learn too much about this matter before it's too late to back out. It will be too late to bow out unscathed if I allow myself to become inextricably involved by being told something I may not want to hear." Acknowledging and imagining potential troublesome eventualities weighed heavily on his mind as he parked his car and walked into the house.

Lucy was sitting at the dining room table reading and answering her e-mail when Daniel walked from the garage into the kitchen. "How you doin'," he asked Lucy as he made his way toward her.

"Just read a message," she offered looking up from the computer terminal, as he stepped toward her, "from my friend in Florida. Says she's selling her house to get away from all those terrible storms they've been having lately. I'm glad she is moving from that area to a more inland location. Oh, how's Ogden doing?"

"Ogden isn't doing so well, I'm afraid. He told me he had been in the hospital several times since I last saw him. Never let me know, of course. I don't know why I would ever think he would tell anyone anything about his problems. That's just like him," Daniel finished somewhat relieved by recalling Ogden's independent trait.

"He's been in the hospital? What on earth has been wrong with him?" Lucy asked as she closed the computer and extended a comforting arm around her husband's waist.

"Cancer. It's an on-going battle, according to what he told me. Started in his prostate and has been spreading. He said his condition is terminal. You talk about being shocked during what I thought was just another casual visit! I wasn't prepared for that news," Daniel stated as he pointedly pulled away from Lucy's arm and rejected her offer of a reassuring embrace as he quickly returned to the kitchen and sat down at the table.

"Oh, my goodness! What terrible news!" Lucy empathized as she walked slowly toward where Daniel sat resting his head in both hands. "I understand how that news would catch anyone unprepared," Lucy said in a consoling voice. "Is there anything we can do for him or Jane?" Lucy had met Ogden's wife soon after Daniel began working with him those many tears ago. They had developed a casual, friendly relationship that had led to meeting for an occasional lunch but their interaction had long since succumbed to mutual inattention.

"Ogden wants me to do some writing for him, Lucy. He wants me to come to his house and record something he feels he needs to get on paper. Other than that, I don't know. Maybe there will be some way we can help them. You know how he is," he offered, anticipating her next likely question.

"You do whatever you can to help him, Dan," Lucy stated, not asking the questions he assumed would follow.

"I will, but you need to know this will probably involve more than one or two visits. I have no idea of how long this will take. I don't know what he wants to record and I don't know why he needs to make a record in the first place," Daniel continued answering unasked questions that he was anxious to have out in the open.

"He asked me not to share whatever he tells me until he gives his consent. I don't know," Daniel talked on, attempting to reassure Lucy while revealing what information he was at liberty to share. "I told him I would help him but I also told him I reserve the right to back off if this becomes beyond my willingness or ability to handle. He agreed with me on that. What do you think?" By stating those facts, Daniel felt assured he had told his wife all he could about his meeting with Ogden Royal.

Lucy paused before she answered, "Ogden feels he needs your help or he wouldn't have asked. I cannot imagine why he would want to be so secretive, but who knows what he needs to tell someone. Did you ever think, considering what he told you about his illness being terminal, that he simply wants your company and a break from thinking about his real problem? I think you should do this for him, Dan," Lucy was now sitting and looking directly at her husband. "As you told Ogden, you may need to re-evaluate the situation as you learn more, but you don't know what you are dealing with at this time. All that may be needed from you is simply to be a friend to a very sick man who needs to talk."

With her unsurprising pragmatic summary, Lucy touched Daniel's shoulder and kissed the top of his head. "Ogden chose you because he likes and trusts you. You do whatever it is you need to do and I'll help you if you need me. When do you see him again to begin work on this project?" Lucy asked.

"He said he'd call me when he's ready for me to come over. Said he will contact his attorney to have a legal paper prepared and, after that, dependent on his health I suppose, he'll call, but who the hell knows when? I told him I won't be calling him. So, at least until I hear from him, I'm on hold."

CHAPTER 4

Ogden Royal had completed two tours of duty in Vietnam and started his third before most people in this part of the world heard of that Southeast Asian nation or could readily locate the small country on a map. As a highly trained combat specialist, he served as an advisor to ARVN units that operated in what was termed I Corps by the US military command. I Corps, one of four designated zones, was the most northerly region of South Vietnam and was the most likely area to encounter regular North Vietnamese Army soldiers. These were the "hardcore" soldiers sent by Ho Chi Minh to train and supply the Vietcong, the pajama-clad, citizen-guerillas of that troubled land. Ogden's embedded service entailed living as his hosts lived, learning their language and eating their food.

Da Nang was south of where the ARVN units Ogden advised often operated. Hue, Da Nang, Chu Lai, My Lai, Duc Pho and Khe Sanh became familiar places to Lt. Royal long before they became part of American military history. Many times, Ogden recounted to Daniel during relaxed moments, he had stood near the DMZ and looked over into North Vietnam while watching the enemy move along trails undetectable by aerial observers. When those long lines inched their way across that theoretical line into South Vietnam, he would advise calling for artillery or mortar rounds to disrupt movement of their re-supply lines. His order for fire support, made through the ARVN unit commander to a distant ARVN artillery unit, was often lackadaisical in execution, and thus arrived too late for effect or, all too often, completely disregarded.

He learned his adopted comrades were not overly motivated to follow his advice or to clash with their enemy. They seemed to operate on the beliefs that "later rather than earlier," was always preferable and "why should defending our country disrupt an otherwise pleasant afternoon?"

The relaxed attitude of the ARVN unit commanders caused Ogden to dream of becoming part of an American Army unit. His desire for different service would eventually come to fruition after two years of advising units wearing the uniform of South Vietnam. Like most American soldiers, Ogden came to lose trust in the very people he was attempting to safeguard against invasion and domination from the communist, totalitarian north. "After all," Ogden thought in the same vein, as would many American who would eventually follow, "how can another nation win freedom and independence for a people who seemingly don't care enough to defend and sacrifice for themselves?" Army Lieutenant Ogden Royal asked himself the question when answered truthfully, spelled an unsatisfactory ending to an ill-advised American intervention.

CHAPTER 5

Ogden called two-weeks later. Daniel drove over the next morning anticipating what he might learn more that would put his mind at ease. Throughout the years they had known each other, Ogden had never invited Daniel to his home. Daniel and Lucy had, on a few occasions, hosted Ogden and Jane for casual meals but for whatever reason, their hospitable effort had not generated a reciprocal invitation.

Ogden and Jane's home, a two-story brick colonial with a three-car detached garage sat on neatly groomed premises indicative of Ogden's penchant for orderliness. "Certainly," Daniel thought as he surveyed the premises, "he hasn't been physically able to maintain this high standard of maintenance himself."

As Daniel slowly placed his old car into park and started to turn the ignition off, he noticed the 173,421 miles displayed on the odometer. He wondered how many more miles of usage the old car would provide. As he opened the door and turned his head, he glanced at the service decal and saw he should have had the oil changed over two-thousand miles ago.

"Sure hope this old rust bucket doesn't drip oil onto their clean concrete driveway," he thought. Stirred by that worry, he considered an alternative place to park. He decided to risk leaving the car parked in the driveway rather than re-parking alongside the county road where the speed limit seemed to be a mere suggestion to harried motorists.

As he stood to stretch for a moment outside the car, his thoughts turned to the quiet that surrounded him. Then he opened the back door on the driver's side to retrieve his notebook and a tape recorder. Daniel had debated about suggesting to Ogden that perhaps a recording of their conversation might be useful. "Well," Daniel continued his internal wrangling, "I'll bring it along. If Ogden doesn't want to make a voice recording, I'll do my best to write whatever he wants to say."

Daniel had just stepped onto the front porch as the door opened. Jane stood there, smiling and said, "Daniel, come in. How are you? It's good to see you again after all this time."

"Thank you. I'm well and it's good to see you. It's been too long since we all got together."

"How's Lucy doing? You know, I've been thinking about calling her, but I've been catching myself coming and going!"

"Lucy keeps busy with her interests and activities. She keeps close contact with the kids and watches over me, which I'm sure she'd tell you, is her biggest job," he replied hoping to disguise his apprehension. "Sometimes I don't see how she keeps up with all her interests. Sure, Jane, when you have time, please call her. I know she would love to hear from you," Daniel stated, now sure his discomfort was evident as Jane directed him toward where he assumed he would find Ogden.

"Dan," Jane continued, nearly whispering, as they made their way down the hallway and to a room located at the rear of the house that he would learn was the study, "I'm glad you were willing to meet with Ogden. He's been looking forward to having you over. I'm sure he'll enjoy talking with someone other than me! He's back here," Jane stepped aside and indicated by a wave of her hand the direction he was to follow.

"I'm pleased he allowed me an opportunity to work with him. I just hope I can be of some help," Daniel said while thinking to himself, "without becoming involved in something beyond my willingness to handle."

"Come in, Dan," Ogden called out in a voice stronger than Daniel remembered when they had last met at Smitty's.

"O.R., where are you hiding?" Daniel asked playfully as he paused at the doorway.

When Daniel entered the room and offered his hand, Ogden adjusted his recliner to an upright position. A small table, not fitting the décor of the room, was leaning against a comfortable chair Daniel assumed was for his usage.

"Have a seat there, Dr. Dan," Ogden pointed toward the chair. "Thought a small table might come in handy and be more comfortable for writing. Nice morning, isn't it? Love this time of year. Not too warm during the day and the cool mornings and evenings, well, better enjoy it before nice and cool turns into too darned cold!" Ogden then sat back and smiled as he thought about, perhaps, those fall days when he fished and hunted or worked in his yard.

Before Daniel sat down, he noticed a display case mounted on the wall over the fireplace. Inside the case was one gold-colored oak leaf that indicated the rank of an Army major. Underneath the oak leaf pin were gold-colored crossed rifles, indicating the holder had been an Army infantryman. A blue and silver-wreathed combat infantryman's badge, a black and gold Army Ranger patch, parachutist's wings, a Purple Heart ribbon and…one other ribbon that riveted Daniel's attention.

"O.R.," Daniel, still standing, turned toward his friend while still pointing toward the one ribbon that had frozen him in his tracks, "is that what I think it is?" Without shifting his posture or his gaze, he continued to point directly at the ribbon that had suddenly captured his interest as he waited for a reply. Though Daniel knew what the ribbon signified, he realized there had to be more about his old friend than he ever imagined existed. He wanted to know what Ogden had done that merited such high military honor signified by that ribbon.

"Well, Dr. Dan, I suppose the answer is entirely dependent upon what you're talking about. I can't imagine why you are standing there looking like a deer caught in the headlights of an oncoming car," he chuckled.

"Ogden, I know what those insignias and ribbons mean and stand for. As you know, I was in the Army, in Vietnam, as an infantry officer. I was never in a Ranger unit but I earned the right to wear the insignia. I didn't serve over there as long as you did, but I was there. You have a Purple Heart for a wound received in battle and you have… a Distinguished Service Cross! My goodness, man, I never knew! How would I know, how would anyone know unless you said something? Here I've been associated with a hero all these years and never had a clue of your past service. Well, I suppose you have your reason for keeping your military service to yourself, knowing how you are about such things. Nevertheless, O.R., I am honored to be in your presence!" Daniel concluded and sat down waiting for Ogden's response.

"Then you are right," Ogden began, "that's what it is. A ribbon. Jane put all those trinkets together after my discharge from the Army. To be honest with you, I've wished many times she'd take the damn thing down and get rid of it. You know, as

Kristofferson sang in one of his songs, 'Yesterday is dead and gone…' That part of my life is many yesterdays ago."

After pausing to collect his thoughts, Ogden continued, "What happened during my time in the military is history and it is over. I didn't join the Army for any personal gain or glory. I wanted to serve this country. That's all," he concluded as he reached for his coffee and waited for a reply.

Daniel studied the wall display as Ogden sat back in his chair and relaxed after his somewhat spirited revelation. "The Distinguished Service Cross," Daniel thought, "is the second-highest military award for heroism, second only to the Medal of Honor. The DSC is awarded for bravery in combat, not for administrative work or for rear echelon personnel, but for actual, confirmed heroism in battle." While he considered what he remembered about military honors, he made a mental note to do a little research when he returned home later that afternoon.

"What about the Purple Heart ribbon, O.R.," Daniel ventured one more question he reasoned might explain the DSC.

"Dan," Ogden suddenly seemed irritated that the discussion had turned to a topic he did not intend to discuss. His voice was thin and strained as he lectured, "Let's put our days of soldiering to rest for now. Yes, I earned a Purple Heart ribbon, as did many other people who served in combat. In my case, I was lucky enough to come out alive and be present for the ceremony. That's all. If one ribbon were a good thing, then wouldn't two ribbons be better? Yes," Ogden surmised, "got 'em both on the same operation," he surmised, obviously wanting to avoid a subject he had never discussed with anyone except, perhaps Jane. "We may get into a little more on this subject later, but that's not why you are here," he stated flatly, reminding his guest he would not tolerate any subsequent attempt to distract him.

"I can sit here and talk for a few more minutes, but as you can see," Ogden paused and shifted himself to a different position, "I am tiring quickly. How about some coffee before we continue?" Ogden asked as he struggled to fill a cup for his visitor.

Upon that terse summation, Daniel dropped the subject of Ogden's military service. He secretly hoped, and intended, to pursue this topic when Ogden was willing to provide more information on a matter he found fascinating. "If he needs or wants to include that part of his life in the story he wants written, that will be his call," he thought as he opened his notebook and retrieved the tape recorder from his case.

When Ogden saw the tape recorder he said, "I'm not comfortable making a taped conversation. I don't mean to be a prick or make this tougher on you than what it may become but, that just won't work for me," he stated in his matter of fact manner.

"I was about to ask you about that," came the prompt offer to explain his intent. "If you don't want to use a recorder, then that's fine with me. Just an idea, not a necessity on my part," he added as he placed the device back inside its carrying case.

"One more thing we need to discuss this morning," Ogden again changed the subject. "I don't have the document I thought I would have ready for you today. I did visit my attorney," Ogden explained, "and he is in the process of preparing that instrument. It should be ready when you come back for our next visit. Hope that doesn't cause you undue concern. I didn't mean to promise and not deliver," his weak voice signaled the meeting was coming to a rapid close.

"That's understandable, O.R. No concern on my part," Daniel offered. "Should we bring this to a close for today and get back together later? You tell me," Daniel said as he noticed the unmistakable signs of weariness.

"We've talked long enough for today," Ogden agreed. "I think I've had enough for now. I'll call you in a few days and see when you can come back over. Don't want to have you make unnecessary trips over here, but I'm not up to a long, drawn-out conversation this morning, as I'm sure you noticed," he replied in a barely audible voice.

"You rest and I'll come back when you call. I apologize for my rambling and wasting our time together. I promise not to make that mistake again. I've enjoyed our meeting. Don't worry. I remember our agreement. What you told me this morning, as far as I'm concerned, will not be shared with anyone. It's, as they say in the business, 'off the record,'" Daniel jokingly reassured his old friend.

"I'll be calling you. Thanks for coming over this morning. What I have to tell you does not involve anything about my military service. That's all a matter of public record. There is absolutely no need to re-hash that part of my life with you or anyone else. So," Ogden brought the conversation toward its end, "what we discussed this morning isn't private or part of our agreement. I think I heard Jane leave a few minutes ago. Can you find your way out?" With that, Daniel realized their first meeting, while interesting and surprising, hadn't addressed any of his concerns or relieved his anxiety.

"Sure, I'll be on my way. I'll be waiting to hear from you. You take care of yourself and please tell Jane I said thanks for the coffee. I hope to see you soon," Daniel said as he made his way out of the room and found his way to the front door and back to his car. He looked underneath his vehicle and was relieved to see clean concrete.

CHAPTER 6

"There's more to Ogden than I imagined," Daniel considered as he drove toward home. He recalled those times when his friend had seemed oblivious to petty concerns that perplexed those who hadn't withstood and survived challenges, which apparently, Ogden had experienced. Daniel hoped to learn more about Ogden's life as a soldier, and a heroic one at that, if Ogden ever agreed to discuss the matter further.

Daniel, who had earned respectable commendation and award for his own military service felt compelled to consult the worldwide web for information concerning the Distinguished Service Cross. He found, as he already knew, the DSC is the second-highest decoration given for "extraordinary heroism for extreme gallantry in action and risk of life in actual combat with an armed enemy force."

He read that out of over 1,000 DSC awards conferred during the Vietnam conflict, 400 were posthumous. One such hero was Hal Moore, then a lieutenant-colonel battalion commander with the First Air Cavalry Division that battled the NVA in the Ia Drang Valley, South Vietnam in 1965. LTC Moore eventually served as an Army general. "Ogden," thought Daniel, "was one of the few recognized heroes of Vietnam and during all the time I've known him, he never breathed a word of it to me or to anyone, as far as I know."

"A few days" turned into three weeks before Ogden called. When he answered the telephone and recognized the voice, Daniel assumed they were about to arrange their next meeting.

"Dr. Dan," Ogden began with his familiar greeting, "I didn't get right back with you as I had planned because I've been down with one aggravation after another. I do have the paperwork from my attorney," and then took what seemed like an unusually long pause before he finished the sentence, "and thought you might want to stop by the house to pick it up."

"Are you doing better now?" Daniel asked, ignoring his suggestion concerning the document.

"I'm coming out of it, but I'm not feeling up to sitting and talking. If you want, stop by the house sometime today or tomorrow. Jane should be home, I think, for both those days, at least during the morning hours. She'll be expecting you and she'll have an envelope for you. Take it home, read it over and we'll go from there and, hopefully, continue our talk soon. I should be back on my feet by the first of next week. Does that work for you?" Ogden posed a direct question.

"Sure, if that's alright with you and Jane, I'll stop over tomorrow morning, say, around nine?"

"I'll let Jane know. Thanks. I'll be in touch." With that, the conversation ended.

"I don't know what he wants to tell me, Daniel considered, "but I better be finding out fast from the way this is going. I don't think he will be willing or able to draw this out much longer." With that realization vexing his mind, Daniel found it difficult to concentrate on other matters for the rest of the day and most of that night. "How and when will this thing ever get started, let alone end?" he repeatedly asked himself as he tossed, then turned and fought sleep.

The next morning, as agreed, he made his second trip to the house on Maple Grove Road. This time he parked on the side of the road making sure his car was clear of passing traffic.

Jane must have been standing by, ready for his visit as she immediately opened the door and greeted him, "Good morning, Dan. Come... in," she stated haltingly as she stepped aside.

Daniel gathered, from Jane's appearance, she hadn't slept well or rested for some time. The fastidious, attractive woman Daniel saw during his last visit and expected to see that morning was now a worried and tired-looking old woman. Hair and clothing, Daniel supposed, were evidently the last concerns on her mind.

"Thanks, Jane. How are you doing? I suppose Ogden told you I was to stop by this morning; at least I hope he did?" he inquired.

"Yes, I have the envelope right here. Ogden said you should take it with you and read what he had drawn up," she added. As she picked the folder up from a nearby table, her hand trembled, causing the thin file to jiggle from side to side, up and down, as if she was unsure what she should do or say. Then suddenly, she turned away, replaced the folder back on the table, sat down on a chair near the front door and wiped her eyes with a tissue she found in the pocket of her bathrobe.

"Is Ogden here? Don't misunderstand the purpose of that question because I don't expect to talk with him this morning. He told me he would have me over, probably next week," he tested.

"Ogden called you from his hospital room. He insisted you have this document from his lawyer while he regains strength. He's still there and will be, we think, until tomorrow," she offered trying to explain her tiredness and appearance and then hurriedly continued, "Ogden had a relapse, a close one this time. I just don't know how much longer he can fight his illness. It seems he grows weaker each day. He wants very badly to complete what he started with you, but who knows? He's a fighter, I know that, but I wonder how much longer he can hold on."

"Jane, you need to take care of yourself. You look tired. Have you eaten anything this morning?" Daniel offered consolation as he continued, "I don't know how you feel right now, nobody but you knows that, but I lost my father to cancer. I do know the pain I felt during that stressful time. You can't get down yourself. If you allow that to happen, Ogden will suffer all the more because he won't have you for support."

"I know. I know...I know I need to take care of myself, but I'm not as strong as Ogden. Guess I buy too many problems that may never happen and worry myself almost to distraction," Jane volunteered as tears began to stream from her eyes.

Then she became more sullen as she suddenly became stern and added, "I just don't think it's a good idea for Ogden to involve you with this writing business, whatever he may want to tell you. Believe me, I've told him what I'm telling you now. For reasons I haven't determined, he insists on going forward. Do you think you could steer him away from going ahead with this?" Jane was becoming more upset the longer she spoke.

"Jane," Daniel began as he recognized he wasn't quite the welcome visitor he had imagined, "I didn't ask Ogden to meet with him and write his story. He asked me for my help," he stated calmly and sincerely. "I think you should have another talk with Ogden," he paused then continued, "because I don't want to play the role of an unwelcome, interfering guest in your home. Believe me; I'll not come back here if that's what you both want. I don't want to do anything against your wishes but I gave Ogden my word," Daniel felt betrayed and irritated by an unexpected, sudden dismissal and rejection of Ogden's request.

"Dan, please, I didn't mean to sound so rude. Please forgive me," Jane began as she moderated her refined southern voice, "but he isn't going to get much better, as you likely know. I don't know if the cancer has or will affect his mind," she added as her voice returned to a more strained pitch. "I am not comfortable with this arrangement. I'll do as you suggested, and I'll talk to Ogden when he gets home from the hospital. Whatever we decide, I'll not confront you about this again. I realize you are simply doing this for your friend," Jane calmly added, "My problem with this isn't about you."

"I appreciate that, Jane," he said considering how frail and weak she looked as she sat crumpled on the chair. "I understand why you are feeling the way you feel. Whatever you and Ogden decide will be fine with me. As I told him when he brought this up," Daniel wanted her to hear once again, "I will help if I can. That's all. If he has a change of mind, or if you feel this should not go forward and Ogden agrees, I'll return this paperwork and we'll part as friends. Is that being fair with you?" Daniel felt he had been kind with his remarks but that he had explained his position in forthright and concise terms.

"We'll talk, Dan. Ogden or I will let you know what we decide," she seemed reassured and relieved she had stated her feelings on the matter clearly and in unmistakable terms.

"I'll be on my way and wait to hear something from the House of Royal," Daniel interjected, attempting to depart on a lighter note. "You go get yourself something to eat and a have cup of coffee. Ogden doesn't want you to become sick from worry about things you can't control. I'll leave you alone so you can eat something and rest. Will you promise me you will try?" he asked as he picked up the envelope from the side table and turned toward the door.

"Thanks for stopping. I'll let Ogden know you were here when I see him later today. I imagine you will hear from us sometime next week. If you are to return, I hope he will be strong enough to sit and talk a little longer than at your last visit," Jane replied with an enthusiasm that had escaped her earlier. Daniel sensed she seemed relieved their brief visit was concluding and that she had shared her misgivings.

"Okay, Jane. You call me anytime you need anything. Lucy asked about you after my first visit here. If you need to talk with another woman, give her a call. She's pulled me through several dark days," he offered as he opened the door in anticipation of a response that never came.

CHAPTER 7

As Daniel pulled away from the edge of the lawn, he thought, "Damn, what a kick square in the ass! Here I am, involved once again in a dumb-assed, half-baked situation I didn't create. Ogden should have discussed this with Jane before he asked me to help him," he continued his internal rant.

"Well," Daniel forced himself to relax when he noticed his knuckles were white from gripping the steering wheel too tightly, "let them work this out. As far as I'm concerned, I'm moving on to something else. I won't worry myself with anything I can't control." As he continued on his way toward home, he remembered those times when he had misjudged Ogden. "Maybe," he concluded, "there is more to this than what I know. I'll just let this take its course. Ogden can deal with Jane. After all," he reassured himself, "I was just trying to do what I had been asked."

Again, the anticipated call from Ogden or Jane was slow in coming. Daniel thought one of them would probably let him know what they had decided sometime early the next week. When one week passed, then two, Daniel began to think the project had been scrapped and Ogden didn't want to make the call that would end their agreement prematurely and likely their association.

Daniel studied his copy of the document Ogden's attorney had prepared. The agreement spelled out what Ogden wanted and expected from him. Again, as Ogden had explained, he would eventually have the right to use the material for his own purpose, *"upon the death of or written release from Ogden Royal."* That release would occur when Ogden's story was completed *and* when the second part of whatever it was Ogden needed him to do was satisfied. That "second part," according to the document, *"will be specified by Ogden Royal at a date to be determined by him, or by his attorney."* The attorney, a high school classmate of Ogden, Thomas Arthur, would be available, if needed, to assist Daniel in the event of Ogden's incapacity. Daniel noticed Ogden had not included Jane in the wording of this contractual matter.

At the bottom of the second page, underneath where someone had stamped "Copy," Ogden had written, "Dr. Dan, if this agreement meets with your approval, you will need to call Tom's office and arrange an appointment so you can sign the original. They will witness and notarize as they see fit. Wait until we meet or talk before you call Tom." This last sentence had been underlined and Ogden had signed with his familiar "O.R."

"Aha," Daniel yielded once again to his earlier suspicion, "He may have sensed this might not meet with Jane's approval." He put that thought from his mind and, once again, reminded himself it might be better for all concerned if Ogden dropped the entire matter.

"Ogden must have gone to some expense in having this document written," Daniel considered. "Lawyers, high school friends or not," he mused, "don't work on matters such as this pro bono." No, if he was determined and serious enough about the completion of this matter that he willingly paid for legal advice and service, he would not be changing his mind without due cause. He would not likely back away, once he had taken this step, simply to please Jane or anyone else. Ogden was never flippant or reckless when it came to spending money, at least in Daniel's presence. He had witnessed

Ogden's trait of strong, determined tenacity when he believed he was doing what was right on more than a few occasions.

"No," Daniel continued to counsel himself, "he intends for this to be finished. He'll work this out with Jane and I'll be hearing from him. I just hope we'll have enough time before he becomes too weak, or incoherent, to say what he wants to say." Once again, he recalled those times he had jumped to the wrong conclusion about Ogden. "I'll learn, someday, not to misjudge him," he chided himself as he placed his copy of the agreement back inside the folder.

"So, have you heard anything from Ogden lately?" Lucy asked as he came down the stairway and into the kitchen.

"No, not a word and it's been almost three weeks now. As I told you, Jane was upset about what Ogden asked me to do. Guess he hadn't told her what he was up to, at least, not completely. It's possible Ogden told her what he plans to tell me and that has given her cause for concern. I don't know what to think." Daniel grumbled as he sat at the kitchen table on his chair that afforded an unobstructed view of their backyard.

"Hey," began Lucy displaying her displeasure with his attitude, "enough of that. Thought you were going to let this take its course. What do you really have to lose? It's nothing to you. You are the one doing all the favors. Get real! I don't want you worked up and frustrated by anything that you can't control in an innocent attempt to do a favor for a friend. You should know better than that!" she added as she brought him a cup of coffee.

"You're right, I should know better. I was simply surprised and caught off guard by Jane's reaction when I stopped to get my copy of the paperwork. Why in the world," he now spoke in a calmer voice, "wouldn't he have at least told her what he doing?"

"You probably know Ogden better than anyone other than Jane," Lucy replied, "and you know how he can be when it comes to revealing anything about his personal affairs or how he feels. The man is borderline mysterious, if you want my opinion. I'm sure," she consoled, "Ogden Royal is a good person and he means well but don't be surprised when he does something like this. Dan, you have known the man for over thirty years, around him every day for over two years and you just learned four or five weeks ago about his military honors. A real secretive guy, again, only my opinion," she emphasized with a reassuring smile.

"Ogden can be remote at times, that's for sure," he agreed as he began to relax. "Let's just leave it at where it's at. If he calls, I'll help. If not, well, at least I did all I was allowed to do for him. I don't have any reason to punish myself. I haven't involved myself in anything where I wasn't welcomed, in the beginning at least. I'm going to work on my column for the weekly paper," he resolved. "I have plenty to do without looking for more problems and distractions. Thank you, Lucy. You always help me see things for what they really are. Without you, I believe I'd go off the rails," he declared as he stood, embraced his wife with one arm and kissed her on her forehead.

The following Monday morning, Daniel was busy, as he had promised Lucy, "working on a column," when he overheard Lucy on the phone, "Well, hello, Jane. It's been awhile since I last spoke with you. I want you to know that I'm here if you ever need anything. Yes. Anytime I can help you. Yes, let me get him. Hang on for a minute. Bye now and you take care of yourself," then Lucy turned and motioned for Daniel to come to the telephone.

"Who is it," Daniel mouthed knowing it was Jane. "It's Jane Royal. She wants to speak with you."

"Hello...Jane," Daniel answered attempting to disguise the hesitancy he felt and his surprise that Ogden wasn't the caller. Again, Daniel suspected Jane to be the wielder of the axe that would sever his relationship with Ogden.

"Dan," Jane began in a hesitant tone, "Ogden and I have had a long talk. We've decided he should continue his project with you. Dan," she sounded chastised, "I'm sorry for the way I acted when you stopped here for the paperwork. I just didn't fully understand Ogden's purpose or what he had in mind. Now I do and I feel terrible about the way I treated you. Will you forgive me?"

"Jane, there's nothing you did that should cause you to feel you need to be forgiven. I know you were upset and I understand why. I appreciate your concern and that you were open and honest with me, he sympathized and continued, "I know you are going through a tough time. Please know I regard both of you as special people, friends, and both of you have earned my unconditional respect."

"Thanks, Dan," Jane continued. "Ogden and I are on the same page with this now. You need not worry about that anymore. Ogden needs to speak with you, so hang on. Give my best to Lucy. Tell her thanks for her offer. I may be calling her. Maybe we can meet sometime for lunch," Jane concluded as she handed the telephone to Ogden.

"Ogden here, Dr. Dan," Ogden began in a cheerful voice. "Sorry about the run-in you had with Jane. It really wasn't her fault. You know me," Ogden was talking freely, "I'm slow to explain what I'm thinking and Jane was left in the dark by a plan she didn't know much about. I told Jane it was just a matter of getting old and forgetful," he added with a discernible chuckle.

"I understand O.R.," Daniel offered as he conveyed the matter was inconsequential by adding muted laughter. "It's water under the bridge, as far as I'm concerned. No harm done."

"Okay, so let's get on with it. You'll need to call Tom Arthur's office and see when you can stop by to sign the agreement. I assume all that met your approval?" Ogden asked.

"Ogden, I think it's fine. I don't fully understand why that was necessary, but it seems fine to me," Daniel stated to alert Ogden he had several immaterial questions he needed answered.

"Dan, you'll have answers to your uncertainties as we get on down the road with this. I understand your concerns, but trust me on this. This will all work out. Call Tom's office, square those details away and, this time, you call me. We'll get together after you see Tom. I think you will enjoy meeting old Tommy. He's quite a guy!" Ogden reminisced.

"Fine, Ogden," Daniel agreed. "I'll call Mr. Arthur's office this morning. Just as soon as I meet with him, I'll call you and you can decide when to have our next meeting. Will that be alright with you and Jane?" Daniel wanted to emphasize the importance of having Jane participate, if she desired, in their future meetings.

"That's the plan, Dr. Dan," Ogden seemed almost jovial. "After...you see Tom, we'll get this show on the road," Ogden once again stressed they would meet *after* Daniel had spoken with Thomas Arthur.

"I'll be calling you, Ogden. You take care and give my regards to Jane. Hope to see you both soon." At least "soon" was what Daniel had in mind as he, this time, concluded their conversation.

CHAPTER 8

As Daniel drove to meet with Thomas Arthur, he thought about lawyers he had known over the years and then about their son, John, who was an attorney in northern Indiana. "For the most part, except for John," Daniel thought, "mostly stuffed white shirts with bugs up their asses," he smiled as he imagined a prissy lawyer walking around wearing thinly soled Italian-made shoes dying to scratch his rear. Daniel recalled something he once read concerning lawyers: "One lawyer in a town will nearly starve. If a second lawyer hangs a shingle in that town, those two bandits will end up owning the entire town!" "Mr. Arthur," Daniel surmised, "isn't likely starving due to the proliferation of lawyers in Bloomington."

When Daniel parked in front of the building located on the rough end of North Rogers Street his first thought was that he had made a mistake and was in the wrong place. After re-checking the address, he was satisfied he had found the correct location. Daniel assumed Arthur would have some type signage, or at least the proverbial shingle, but his visual survey proved his assumption wrong. "I would think that a big-shot lawyer would want to display some noticeable mark that might attract more business. But, then again, why would any lawyer worth his salt want his office in this part of town?"

Daniel decided to go inside and ask if anyone could help him locate Arthur's office. Daniel opened the outside door and walked into a poorly lighted entryway made dimmer by walls painted a brown-tone that reminded him of mud. He noticed a light shining through the glass window of an office at the far end of the dank hallway. "Maybe someone in there has some idea where I can find Thomas Arthur," Daniel coached himself.

"Excuse me," Daniel said in a whispered voice to gain the attention of a casually dressed younger woman sitting behind a computer terminal as he stepped halfway inside the door, "I'm looking for Thomas Arthur's office. Can you steer me in the right direction?"

Before the typist could look up to answer, a drawling, friendly voice seemed to echo from the rear of the office, "Daniel Tyler, is that you? Get your route-stepping self in here! You've found me, you super-sleuth!"

"What? Well…yes, I'm Dan Tyler. I need to see Mr. Arthur," he stammered, surprised by such an enthusiastic greeting from someone he couldn't see and hadn't met.

"Daniel Tyler, I'm Tom Arthur," the lawyer offered as he stepped toward Daniel with his hand extended, all the while smiling as if he had heard or just finished telling a humorous story.

Thomas Arthur was not wearing thinly soled Italian-made footwear. Arthur appeared to be the opposite of any lawyer Daniel had ever encountered or had concocted in his mind. Arthur was wearing blue jeans, a red sweatshirt and cowboy boots. Thomas Arthur stood well over seventy-eight inches tall and was as lean and chiseled as if he worked six days every week performing manual labor. A moustache and goatee drew Daniel's gaze from Arthur's cleanly shaven head.

"Come on back, Dan," Arthur gestured, indicating the route Daniel should follow. "Come in, grab a chair and we'll talk for a few minutes. Hell," Arthur smiled, "you're here on old Ogden's dime, so why be in any hurry?" Arthur laughed as he stroked his moustache.

"I called your office earlier to see when I should stop by to sign a document Ogden Royal had you prepare. I was told to come in at this time," Daniel offered, stating the obvious.

"Yes, I know. How's Ogden holding up? Didn't appear too chipper when he stopped in here a few days ago," Arthur added in a somber tone as he returned to his chair, leaned back and placed his booted feet on the edge of his desk.

"I don't know. I did speak with him a few days ago when he called me at home. He sounded almost like the old Ogden. It's been two months, or so, since I actually saw him. You say you saw him a few days ago? Well, you have seen him more recently than I," stated Daniel.

"Let me tell you a few things, Dan, about old Ogden you might not know," Arthur began as he removed his feet from the desk and leaned slightly forward. "We went through high school together at the old Bloomington High School down on Second and Walnut, Class of 1954. Well, back then, I must have epitomized what the kids now call a jerk, at least a misfit. Didn't give a hoot about athletics, wasn't all that handsome, sure as hell couldn't dance or sing. I was just a damn good student when I wanted to be with a mouth that overloaded my ass a few times, if you get my drift," Arthur smiled.

"But Ogden," Arthur continued his remembrance, "that bastard was the toughest dude who ever put on a Panther wrestling uniform. Naw, he wasn't a big feller, as you can imagine, not at all, but he sure as hell was determined when he got on that wrestling mat with someone. Hell, man, Ogden was undefeated his entire junior year and won the state championship. Same thing his senior year, undefeated right through the semi-final match of the state meet. He won as a semi-finalist all right. But the unfortunate rascal had to forfeit the championship match that night because he had broken a bone in his wrist during the morning event!" Arthur shook his head in amazement. "Can you imagine not *just* finishing a wrestling match, but winning it… with a broken wrist? You tell me, is that one tough bird, or what?" Arthur exclaimed.

"No, I have never heard anything about Ogden's high school wrestling success or anything about his military record until about two months ago. Ogden isn't exactly a walking billboard when it comes to talking about himself, at least he isn't to me," Daniel stated.

"You know, I wasn't one bit surprised when I heard Ogden had volunteered for all that specialized Army training. Knowing him as I do, I cannot imagine Ogden Royal doing anything half-assed. It's just not in his nature to go at anything he determines worthwhile less than full bore," Arthur characterized his classmate.

"Ogden is one of a kind. I really haven't had a lot of interaction with him, just the occasional cup of coffee or a round of golf. We have never been together socially for more than an hour or two at a time for any reason. I do, however, regard him with the utmost respect, I can tell you that," Daniel stated. "Hard to determine what he's thinking sometimes, but he has always been a good friend to me," he concluded.

"Ogden will relate just whatever he figures someone needs to know," offered Arthur. "Well," he continued, "we do have a bit of business to attend to." Arthur seemed to become officious, as he asked, "You've read Ogden's agreement, I suppose? Do you have any questions I can answer?" While asking those questions, he pulled several pages of documentation from a file.

"No. It all seems as Ogden had explained to me before he came to see you," Daniel answered.

"Grace, will you and Paul please step in here for a minute? Need you guys to witness old Dan's signature," Arthur announced loudly enough to gain prompt response from his assistants.

"Daniel Tyler," Arthur continued as the woman Daniel had spoken to before meeting Arthur, entered his office, "this is my daughter, Grace. This young feller here is my son, Paul," Arthur beamed proudly. "Grace," Arthur explained, "is a fine young lady and a damn good trial lawyer. She's almost as good as her old man! Paul, this young scamp here, is in law school and hangs out with his sister and old man learnin' lawyerin' when he's not hiding out over at Third and Indiana buried in some stuffy law book or listening to a silver-tongued, non-practicing professor hold forth on one theory or another," Arthur chuckled as Grace and Paul smiled before seating themselves.

"Grace, Paul," Daniel said offering his hand to each, "pleasure to meet you both."

"Well, let's get it done. Daniel, you need to sign here and initial at those two places," Arthur indicated with his pen. "These two young shysters will witness your John Hancock," Arthur smiled looking kindly at his children. "Grace, please give Dan here his copy of the signed agreement before he leaves. You'll have plenty of time to do that, so no big rush. Daniel and I need to discuss another matter before he escapes the premises," Arthur stated in a matter-of-fact tone.

"What... other matter... do you have in mind that we need to cover, Mr. Arthur?" Daniel asked as Grace and Paul departed and returned to their desks. "What else is there to discuss?" Daniel asked somewhat unnerved by Arthur's statement.

"Yeah, Ogden and Jane have requested I ask you to perform another service for them, Dan. They have asked for your help with another matter they are concerned about," explained Arthur.

"What else can they possibly need from me?" Daniel asked looking directly at the lawyer begging clarification for what had been a surprising addendum to their meeting.

"Dan, call me Tom. Why so damn formal? If you made the cut to be considered a friend by Ogden Royal, you are damn well sound enough fabric to be on a first name basis with the likes of me," Arthur stated with emphasis as he retrieved two other documents from a file lying on his desk.

"Here's the deal, Dan," Arthur continued, as he closed the folder, "Ogden and Jane want to appoint you as executor of their estate and...want you to exercise their general and medical powers of attorney in the event either of them is deceased or incapacitated. In other words, as long as either of them is able to act on behalf of the other, you remain out of the mix. However, if either of them dies or is determined incompetent, you will be at bat. How does that strike you?"

"It strikes me as one big surprise, Tom. Ogden didn't say a word about this to me. And for Jane to make this request, well, I'm shocked, to say the least," Daniel replied while trying to mentally process what Tom Arthur had announced. "Ogden, I can understand to a point," continued Daniel, "but Jane? I didn't expect anything like this from her. You talk about a shot coming from left field!" Daniel stated as he sat back in his chair.

"You got it right, partner," Arthur smiled. "Both of 'em. You're the man they want handling their estate, hell, maybe even the guy who will pull the plug, so to speak. They both must think highly of you and trust your judgment." Arthur surmised. "Well, what are you thinking, Dan? You gonna do it or not? It's up to you to run, pass, punt or carry the ball. Ogden and Jane are offering you the ball. I have these documents all ready to go, in their final form, pending your approval and acceptance. You certainly do not have to serve in this capacity. It's your call," Arthur said as he clasped his hands on the desktop and waited for Daniel to answer.

"Tell me this, Tom," Daniel asked searching for direction and clarification, "do they not have a family member that should be considered for these important matters? I know they don't have children, but a brother, a sister, cousin, some relative somewhere that might contest involvement from someone outside the family?"

"No, they do not. They don't have any close relatives, anywhere. Well, Jane said she does have a distant cousin, a third or fourth, she wasn't sure how closely they are related, who lives in Wyoming, but they have not even exchanged so much as a Christmas card over the years. Wouldn't recognize each other if they were both standing in line waiting for a seat at Nick's. Haven't seen each other in over forty years, according to Jane. No, Dan, you shouldn't be concerned with anyone raising a ruckus in the event you do actually need to exercise these instruments. Anyway, you'll have the full power and legal expertise of Thomas, Grace and Paul Arthur backing you up and legally kicking anyone's ass who even thinks of causing a problem," Tom offered as he smacked the desk lightly to indicate his resolve.

"Okay, Tom. Yes, then I'll do it!" Daniel felt relieved Tom had evidently thoroughly discussed other possible candidates with the Royals before they had agreed he would be their best choice.

"Then it's a done deal, Dan," smiled Arthur. You have made a very good decision and Ogden and Jane will be pleased. There's nothing else for you to sign. I'll keep copies of their wills and medical POA's here in my office. We'll mail you copies of both instruments for your file. Do you have other questions for me?" Tom asked.

"Just one more, if I may," Daniel began. "Not meaning to sound overly inquisitive, but are matters such as wills and estates your usual practice?"

"Oh, you've noticed our lovely, little rat hole of an office, have you?" Tom laughed. "Well, I, rather we, to include Grace, practice as criminal defense attorneys. We don't need a big fancy office. Our clients usually contact us after they've been arrested and are taking a break in some county jail. They don't visit us, before or after their trial. We meet them in just about every foul-smelling county lock-up throughout Indiana and the Midwest. I don't often grab-ass around with such matters as wills and estates, to be honest with you. I did this because Ogden asked me. You can rest assured we are competent in such matters but, although as I said, this is not our major source of income," explained Arthur.

"Criminal law?" Daniel stated inviting Arthur to continue.

"Yep. You may find it unbelievable as I sit here this morning, but I am one kick-ass barrister inside a courtroom," Tom smiled widely as he continued. "Those shit-kickers who sit on most juries feel real comfortable and relaxed when old Tom ambles over to the jury box and pleas with them to spare the life of some low-life bastard that I would shoot myself if given an opportunity. Guess they like my manner," Tom laughed, "or maybe it's because I'm just so darn handsome!"

"Sounds as if you enjoy your work," Daniel, now at ease, smiled as he began to shuffle with his notecase to indicate he was ready to depart whenever Tom felt he had over-stayed his welcome or that their business had been concluded.

"Sure. I've defended some of the most notorious scum bag killers and rapists throughout ten states. Didn't win 'em all but none 'em got the guillotine as many of them really deserved, in my opinion.

"I might add, before I leave you with a flippant summary of our practice, we take our calling very seriously. I consider the mission of a criminal defense lawyer, above all else, to be a protector of the Constitution. Just because the government brings charges and proclaims a person guilty does not make it so.

"We stand by the accused and force the state to prove, beyond reasonable doubt, that the facts warrant the charge. We defend people who are guilty most of the time but, guilty, innocent or not guilty as charged, it is our duty, my calling, to make the law work as intended."

"Thanks, Tom. This has been an interesting and, to say the least, a surprising morning. It's a pleasure to have met you and your children. Thanks again," Daniel stated as he stood up and offered his hand to Thomas Arthur.

"Dan, you know where you can find me. Call anytime we can help you. Don't forget to take your copy of the agreement Grace has ready for you. Give Ogden and Jane my regards. And, Dan..." Arthur paused as he glanced at his ringing telephone, "we'll be meeting again. There will be other matters that I'm sure we'll need to discuss."

CHAPTER 9

"What else am I to learn about Ogden Royal? Why does Tom Arthur believe it will be necessary for me to see him again to discuss 'other matters,'" Daniel mulled as he drove away from Arthur's office. "What other feats has Ogden accomplished that will, for good measure, provide yet another piece of what is becoming a complicated puzzle?" Daniel thought. He continued to consider Ogden, "After I come to the point where I begin to think I've learned all there is to know about him, I may finally discover he walks across Lake Monroe for exercise. At least, he might have," added Daniel, "before he became ill."

As Daniel enumerated Ogden's known accomplishments, he began to compare himself to his friend. "I don't have much in common with Ogden," Daniel admitted to himself. "My paltry military accomplishments compared to a Distinguished Service Cross? That's laughable. My Purple Heart, though I was wounded in combat, I wasn't crippled or disabled, thankfully, to the extent as Ogden. Again, I'm not in the same league, not comparable. Sure, I survived over forty-five air-mobile combat assaults, and have an Air Medal to prove it. Ogden won the state championship as a wrestler when he was a junior in high school, and was undefeated his senior year until he had to forfeit due to injury. I have done nothing that compares, even remotely, to Ogden!" Daniel became morose as his inadequacies and failures weighed on his mind.

By his own appraisal, Daniel was a dismissal failure at everything he had undertaken. While he had served as an effective Army officer, even as an infantry company commander, whatever degree of success he had earned turned out, in hindsight, never enough for Daniel to walk away satisfied. There was always that "someone" who had accomplished more.

Whenever he remembered why he had received a Bronze Star instead of a Silver Star, he would become angry and bitter. He had been recommended for that higher citation but his battalion commander decided his act of valor wasn't worthy of such recognition and had used his influence to intervene.

His conflict with that particular superior officer began one day when the commander visited Daniel's company location in the field. The first words out of the man's mouth were to ask, "Why in hell aren't your men cleanly shaven and more presentable?"

Daniel quickly replied that their water supply was so short they barely had enough to drink let alone enough for shaving. The commander, not willing to accept that as a plausible reason, pressed the issue. Finally, Daniel became angry and replied that if the commander wanted the men to be dressed for an inspection, then he should get them all out of the damned field to a rear area where they could take a shower, shave and change their clothes. Until that happened, his men wouldn't be using what little drinkable water they had for shaving.

With that, the officer stalked away leaving behind his operations officer, a West Point graduate, who got up in Daniels face and snarled, "You know, I'm not surprised that a ROTC officer would talk to his superior officer the way you just did. You can damn well be thankful I'm not the battalion commander because I'd have your ass up on a charge of insubordination! What do you think of that Lieutenant Tyler?"

"I don't give a rat's ass what you think or what he thinks, Captain. How much combat command time have you had? Have you ever commanded an infantry platoon, let alone a company in a combat situation? We've been out here over twenty-five days and our asses are dragging. We're short on water, sir, that's the bottom line. If he wants these men ordered to shave, then he should relieve me of command because I sure as hell won't do it. What do you think of that, Captain, sir? Is that insubordinate enough for you?"

"This is not finished, Lieutenant," the Captain hissed as he toadied back to where his leader was waiting for a helicopter to take them back to their air-conditioned command post located on the battalion firebase.

The captain kept his word. The incident wasn't over and it cost Daniel a Silver Star. At the time, he didn't really care because he had stood up for his men. Over the years when he recalled that ridiculous incident, he wished he had knocked that prick captain flat on his pompous and circumstantial ass.

Daniel had worked long hours at various endeavors after he and Lucy were married. Job after job never seemed to result in the success he had envisioned or expected from himself. While Lucy and the children were never without whatever they needed, Daniel had wanted to provide more for them. Soon after they were married, they purchased a comfortable house in a nice middle-class neighborhood surrounded by solid, hard-working folks much like themselves. In Daniel's mind, their house wasn't large enough or nice enough. The neighbors? Well, they were to remain strangers as far as he was concerned. "I was never satisfied," he reminded himself, "with any job, house, car or much of anything else. Lucy, true, dear and steady Lucy, has been my only source of satisfaction. Even my children," he admitted to himself, "would rather be around almost anyone other than spend time with me. How did I fail so miserably with my own children? Did the children interpret my constant searching and self-loathing as negative feelings toward them?"

He hammered and flailed at himself. "I've wasted my life dissatisfied, not so much as with other people, or with things. I've been dissatisfied with only one thing, one person. I've made myself miserable, as I have long suspected but did not, would not admit to myself up until now. I am the sole source and cause of my misery!" Daniel again vowed he would concentrate on optimistic thoughts and not allow his tendency toward the negative to control his life. "It's not that I'm undisciplined," he reminded himself, "it's just the one thing I've never been able to resist is to kick my own ass, deserved or not, at every possible opportunity."

"Could Ogden and Jane, by naming me as their executor, involving me with writing Ogden's story, insisting on a vow of secrecy... might all this present an opportunity for me to accomplish something truly worthwhile?" he began to think in a positive vein. "Who knows what other surprises Ogden will reveal," Daniel reminded himself. "Perhaps I'm not as washed up as I have been telling myself. This may be my last, best chance. Ogden Royal may be my path to self-redemption and some degree of satisfaction," he counseled himself as he relaxed his grip on the steering wheel and tuned the radio to the mid-day news.

Lucy wasn't surprised to hear Ogden and Jane had named him as executor of their estate. "Without family, they need someone they trust, and you, apparently fill that bill, Dan," Lucy offered. "You should call Ogden this afternoon. Let them know you have talked with their attorney. See when you can meet with them and get this show on the road for your own peace of mind. What do you think?" asked Lucy in her unobtrusive manner she hoped would spur Daniel to make the call he had promised he would make.

"Yes," he agreed, "right now. Keep the ball rolling, eh," he nudged Lucy while scooting away from the table and stepping toward the telephone.

"Jane, how are you? Dan here," he began while still smiling at Lucy.

"Dan, sure," Jane replied in a sleepy-sounding voice. Ogden is napping right now. Just woke up a few minutes ago myself."

"Sorry if my call interrupted your nap," offered Daniel apologetically.

"No… no. Not at all. I was already up and had started going through the mail," Jane seemed to be regaining awareness.

"The reason I called," he reminded Jane, "was to let you and Ogden know I have met with Mr. Arthur. Ogden asked me to call after that meeting."

"Sure, Dan. That's good. You know, Ogden has been much better the past few days. He's felt much better, much stronger. I'll not bother him right now. He needs to rest. I think tomorrow morning, if that's okay with you, would be fine for Ogden. We'll both plan to be home and he will be pleased to see you. Would tomorrow around ten o'clock be convenient for you?" Jane answered acknowledging the purpose of the call.

"Ten, tomorrow morning works for me. I'll be there. Thanks, Jane. Give Ogden my regards. See you tomorrow," he replied, assuming their conversation concluded.

"One more thing, Dan, before you hang up," Jane interrupted. "Ogden and I need your guidance and experience with getting rid of one of our cars."

"Sure. How can I help you with that?" he asked, thinking surely Ogden and Jane weren't selling a vehicle motivated by a need to raise money. "At least," he studied to himself, "Ogden, ever frugal, never seemed to live above his means. And," Daniel recalled, "If they were pressed for cash, how could they afford that beautiful, expensive house they call home?" He quickly dismissed financial difficulty as a plausible explanation for their plan.

"Ogden would like you to find out how much we should ask for a car we want to sell. We are not trading this car for another vehicle. We don't need or want another car. He wants to find out how much we can expect to get for our 2007 Mercedes," Jane continued.

"Tell me about the car. I'll do a little research before I come over tomorrow," Daniel offered as he paced a notepad on the counter and clicked his pen.

"Well," Jane replied thoughtfully, "it's a 2007 model, as I said before, Mercedes E-350, maroon. Has about every extra feature available, I suppose. A very nice car," she added.

"Do you know how many miles are on the car?"

"Let's use about five-thousand. I'm sure it doesn't have any more than that. We bought it new in Indianapolis right before Ogden became ill. We haven't driven the car much, obviously. Ogden just hasn't been out very often and I always drive my car, just out of habit. He thought he just had to have that car, that one luxury, but you know, with what has been going on with him…" Jane's voice trailed without completing what she was thinking.

"Okay, I'll do a little searching and have a price range for you to consider tomorrow. Is there anything else?" He asked before he repeated his earlier mistake by attempting to end the conversation prematurely.

"No, Dan. That's about it for now. See you tomorrow, then. Bye now," she concluded in a tone of voice that indicated she was pleased he had called.

"That was easy enough," he confirmed to Lucy as he replaced the receiver. "Guess I'm becoming gun shy when it comes to dealing with those two," Daniel admitted.

"What was all that discussion about a car?" Lucy inquired.

"They have a car they don't need and want to sell outright, at least that's what Jane said. She asked me to help them determine how much money they should ask a private buyer. Sounds like a darn nice car, a Mercedes no less. I didn't know they had such a vehicle. When I met Ogden at Smitty's, he was driving a small, older suv," Daniel answered.

CHAPTER 10

Jane opened the door before Daniel stepped onto the front porch. "Come on in. Ogden is right where you left him the last time you were here." He could not avoid noticing she was obviously in a more cheerful and positive frame of mind compared to the last time they met.

"Dr. Dan," came the familiar and strong greeting as he stepped into the now-familiar room as offered Ogden his hand, "come in and find yourself a seat."

"You are looking chipper this morning. Good to see you O.R.," he replied as he placed his notebook on the table and sat down. Before inviting further comment, he opened his notebook to indicate he was prepared to fulfill the purpose of their meeting. He would not derail this meeting by asking questions concerning matters that Ogden did not want to discuss or were not relevant.

"So, how did you and Tom get along?" Ogden asked with a hint of mirth in his voice.

"Thomas Arthur is one interesting individual, to say the least. That fellow is almost as interesting as you are! You know, you two," Daniel smiled toward Jane then Ogden, "caught me completely off-guard when Mr. Arthur brought up your request for me to serve as your executor."

"Listen, Dan," Ogden began, "Tom called after you left his office. We know you accepted and we thank you for that. Believe me when I tell you, we appreciate your willingness to help."

"Yes, and you have my thanks as well," Jane added. "While you two guys get on with your talk, I'll make some coffee. I'll be around, so call me if you should need anything else," she offered as she stood and left the room.

"Where do we begin, O.R.? I did put together some pricing information on the car Jane mentioned yesterday, whenever you want to discuss that."

"Yes. The car," Ogden mused. "We don't need a third vehicle. We may as well get rid of it as soon as possible. It just sits getting older and eating up insurance premium. We both have a vehicle besides the Mercedes. I bought that car because I always wanted a very nice car. Well, it is all that, for sure. But, due to circumstances," he stated in a thoughtful voice as he looked away, "we simply do not need to keep it any longer. How much is she worth?"

"According to what I learned from the internet, and from a phone call to a friend still in the business, your car should bring between $27,300 and $31,000 if you plan to sell to a private party," he said as he handed Ogden the numbers he had written on a slip of paper.

"Still worth a pretty penny, then, but not nearly what we paid for it a short time ago," Ogden said almost inaudibly as he placed the scrap of paper on the table by his chair. "Jane," Ogden called out in a clear voice, "bring Dan the keys to the car and the garage door. Ogden lowered his voice, "If you want, go out to the garage and take a look at the car. Look it over, inside and out. See what you think about your price estimate. You worked several years in that business and I'd value your opinion after you've had a chance to make a close inspection," Ogden finished as Jane entered the room and handed Daniel a ring of keys.

When he opened the side door to the garage and flipped the light switch on, Daniel noticed the garage was spotless from ceiling to floor. The car Jane drove was near the side door and the vehicle Ogden had driven to Smitty's occupied the middle lane. Both vehicles were spotless. The Mercedes sat at the far side of the garage covered with white cotton sheets.

He carefully pulled the covers away from the car and laid them aside. As he opened the driver's door, the unmistakable smell and crispness of a new vehicle assailed his senses. Though now two model years old, he realized the vehicle was practically as fresh as the day Ogden drove it home from the dealership.

Daniel inserted the key and turned the ignition to the point where the mileage number on the odometer became readable. "No, Jane, you were off a bit when you guessed five-thousand miles as an estimate," Daniel smiled to himself. The 723 miles on the odometer established why the car emitted the aura of a new model.

As Daniel pecked on the back door and jiggled the handle to announce his presence, Ogden hurriedly closed an envelope as he looked up and asked, "Well, did you take a good look at the car?"

"That is a very beautiful machine! Jane told me yesterday as she described the car over the phone, she thought it had around five-thousand miles on it. She was a little high with that estimate. It shows just over seven-hundred miles, Ogden. Your car is worth a little more than my estimates, due to far fewer miles than I used in my appraisal.

"I left it as I found it. After looking it over, inside and out, I covered it back over with the sheets," he said as he handed Ogden the key ring and sat down.

"We'll talk more about the car when Jane is finished with whatever she's doing. Let's get on with me talking and with you with writing. I have quite a bit to tell you, so let's begin to make a dent in this deal," Ogden stated as he sat back in his chair.

"I'm ready whenever you want to begin," Daniel replied as he re-opened his notebook.

"I used to do a lot of walking just to keep active. With this game leg, I can't run and I won't pay for a health club membership that I probably wouldn't use. So, I found walking at a comfortable pace to my liking. Of course, it's not safe to walk along the roadway, or most streets, so I used to walk around the I.U. football stadium after I was finished with work. Convenient location for me as it is on my way home. Plenty of parking available there and not overly busy or crowded. I found it to be an all-around enjoyable place for me to walk and sort through my thoughts. Before they messed the place up with those abutments and that damned parking lot on the west side, it was, almost exactly, an unimpeded one-half mile around. I might walk maybe three, four or more laps. Walk and think, then head for home." He paused as Jane poured coffee.

"I understand exactly what you are saying. I've walked around Memorial Stadium many times myself. It is a shame they excavated all the trees and tore up the beautiful lawn on the west side of the stadium and paved it over for another parking lot," Daniel agreed.

"One July evening in 1986, I was making what I intended to be my last round of the evening. By that time, it was beginning to get dark. I had made it around to the west side when I just happened to notice an over-sized, dark-green gym bag lying in one of those gullies underneath a tree. I don't think I would have noticed it at all if not for the brass eyelets catching what little light that managed to shine through from the setting sun.

I decided I would walk back to my car and drive around to see if anyone might be around and searching for misplaced property. I drove two laps around the stadium hoping to find the owner," he continued, "but I didn't see another soul on the premises."

With that, he leaned forward to take a drink of coffee. "Am I talking too fast for you? If I do get to going too fast, slow me down," Ogden offered.

"Go ahead. You're doing fine and I'm keeping up, so far," he replied and considered where this story was leading.

"Not seeing anyone, I decided to take a closer look at the bag. After all, it could have been anything from a torn, dilapidated old satchel to some kid's book bag. I decided to park and walk down for a closer look. Remembering some of my military training, I took a length of rope with me. I wasn't about to grab onto anything without taking some basic precaution. You know, with all these students around here," Ogden laughed, "it could have been a bag full of crap or, who knows, poisonous snakes!"

"After a few tugs on the rope I had carefully attached," he now seemed animated by recounting this incident, "I added a few prods with a stick I found lying close by. Nothing inside moved and better yet, nothing exploded. I could tell by the tension on the rope, the bag was nearly full of something as it was quite heavy and didn't move easily. By the time I decided the bag was safe to handle, it was almost dark. I loaded the thing into the trunk of my car and headed home. I thought there might be something inside that would help me locate the owner, but that would have to wait until the next day. I planned to examine the contents after I arrived home, and then consider how best to handle the situation," he stopped as Jane returned and sat down.

"How far did he take you, Dan?" she asked. "Did I overhear him mention his arrival home with the bag inside the trunk of his car?" she offered confirming she already knew the details of the story Ogden was relating.

"Yes. That's where we are now," Daniel managed a quick, confirming glance in her direction as he continued writing.

"Let's take a break and talk about the car for a few minutes," Jane volunteered switching to a subject Daniel assumed had been concluded. "You guys look as if you might need a break in the action," she teased as she stroked her husband's arm. Before she sat down, Jane handed Ogden a large brown envelope.

"So," Ogden began as Jane sat closely at his side, "you said you think the Mercedes should be worth, what did you say, something near thirty-thousand dollars?"

"Sure, your car is worth something pretty close to that. Give or take a few hundred."

"Would you and Lucy like to have the car, Dan?" Jane asked, startling him with a question that was without reason or foundation that he could discern. What had he said that indicated he wanted or was interested in buying their car?

"Want it? While I might want it, I can't afford to buy a car anything like that! Look at what I'm driving," he replied, with a forced chuckle that revealed his agitation. Caught off-guard and sensing he had unwittingly become their clueless jester, he nervously collected his notes and shuffled them inside his notebook. "I can't believe these people thought I wanted to buy their car. Is that why they asked me, baited me, to help them determine an asking price? Sent me out to the garage..." his thoughts were now racing.

"Dan," Jane said in a calming tone as she touched his hand, "you can afford the car. Go ahead and tell him, dear," she said as they smiled and showed they were pleased about something their uncomfortable guest could not fathom.

"Dr. Dan, we have decided to sell you the Mercedes. That's the bottom line. We have the paperwork all prepared and ready to go. Jane, hand me the title and the paperwork Tom put together," Ogden said in his business-like manner familiar to Daniel.

"Ogden, Jane…hey, please, both of you…please… slow down…just a minute here!" Daniel continued to plea. "I'm in no position to buy your car, or any car, for that matter. What gave you any idea I wanted to do such a thing?" he blurted out in a forceful tone that did not disguise his uneasiness. He fought to avoid eye contact as he nervously toyed with his notebook as his thoughts swirled around how he would extricate himself from a situation he did not understand or want to pursue.

"Hey Dan, you wait just a minute before you get too far down the trail of telling us what you can and cannot do. You haven't heard the deal we are offering you yet. Before we told you how much we're asking for the car, you concluded it would be beyond your means. Now, you slow down a bit and relax. Do you have ten-dollars in your pocket?" Ogden asked as he smiled toward Jane.

"Of course, I have ten-dollars but I don't have thirty-thousand bucks," he was now less certain he had become the source and target of their late-morning amusement as he squirmed inwardly, feeling chastised for yielding to an unsupported assumption.

"Then you have what we are asking you for the car," Jane replied as she smiled and playfully patted her husband on his hand.

"What? What… are you two talking about? Ten-dollars for…that car?" he sputtered as he stood up and walked toward the door before he turned and faced his tormentors.

"Come back in here," Ogden beckoned as he began to laugh. Sit back down. You see, Jane and I both noticed you would need a better car before too long. Here," Ogden handed Jane the envelope he had hastily closed when Daniel returned from the garage.

"Dan, it's your car for ten-dollars. We had Tom draw up the bill of sale. It's all legal and both our signatures have been notarized," Jane explained. "We want you and Lucy to have the car," she added with a smile.

"I don't know what to say. Ogden, Jane, I can't allow you to practically give me a car. For ten-dollars? No way is that reasonable. I may be poor compared to you, but I cannot accept such a gift. Thanks for thinking of me, but please…" Daniel continued to berate himself as he realized that, once again, he had misjudged these two well-intentioned, kind people.

"This is not intended as a gift," Ogden stated firmly and continued, "You aren't being given anything. The car represents a partial payment, a retainer, perhaps, for the services you will provide. Jane and I," Ogden said as he held Jane's hand, "prefer to pay as we go."

Jane handed the envelope to Daniel and said, "Ogden and I want you to have the car. It's not a gift. As Ogden just said, it's a retainer. With this upfront payment, we are saying we intend to employ you, that's all."

Daniel hesitated as he took the envelope from her hand, as his gaze darted from Ogden then to Jane before he began, "I didn't agree to do anything for you in expectation of any sort of payment. I can't imagine how I will ever earn this much money for any service you will gain from me," he paused and continued softly, "I accept and I thank you both. This has caught me without words to express how this makes me feel."

"Had you goin,' didn't we, Dr. Dan?" Ogden laughed attempting to lighten what had become a heavy encounter. "I thought there for a minute you were shuffling to the door, ready to jump!" he added resorting to military jargon.

"You sure did, Ogden. I didn't have a clue about what was going on with you two. I kept trying to think if I had said anything that might have led you to believe I was financially able and ready to buy your car," he summarized his earlier, puzzled thoughts.

"Now that the car deal has been settled," Jane declared, "we can move on to other concerns."

"Not today, Jane," Ogden seemed to be tiring after his few minutes of merriment had been brought to a satisfactory conclusion. "I'm getting pretty tired. Dan, take the paperwork and owner's manual with you. Have the title transferred to you and Lucy and get a license plate. Of course, as you well know, you'll need to have the car added to your insurance policy. We'll keep your car safe in the garage until you get those matters handled. Next time you come over, you can take 'er home with you."

"I'll do that. You know, I'm gonna try real hard not to allow anything you two say or do alarm or shock me again. Today, the deal with the car was my comeuppance. I'm a slow learner, but I'm learning! I'll try to be braced for whatever you guys have in store for me," Daniel said, having mustered his composure.

"Don't be too sure about that, Dr. Dan. You haven't heard the whole story yet," Ogden counseled as he reclined and closed his eyes.

"Dan," Jane offered as she walked toward the front door with him, "can you come back over the day after tomorrow, around the same time? Ogden has to see his doctor tomorrow but the day after should be fine."

"Sure, I'll plan to be back here Wednesday. Take care and thanks again, Jane. Hope to see you soon," he offered as he closed the door.

CHAPTER 11

"Sure, I'm pleased about the car, but Ogden and Jane must be expecting a lot from you or they wouldn't have felt obligated to give you anything like that!" Lucy observed after Daniel recounted his morning.

"They don't feel they are giving me anything, and they certainly were not obligated, Lucy," Daniel reiterated becoming agitated and impatient. "I don't know why they sold us their car for ten-dollars other than what they told me. You can accept what they said or you can worry about their reasoning and motives, if you want.

"I'm not going to second-guess and fret about this for one more second. If you don't want to drive the car, well, that's your call as well. In my opinion," he continued in a calmer voice, "we can use a better car, that's for sure. After all, I am providing a service for them. Who knows? Maybe this retainer, as Ogden called it, won't be nearly enough for what might be involved. I don't know, but I do know I don't want you to worry yourself about it," Daniel offered to console his wife.

"When do you plan to go to the license bureau?" Lucy asked as excitement overcame her initial bewilderment and hesitation.

"I'll go this afternoon," he replied becoming agreeable as he stood and gently embraced his wife while hating himself for yielding to the heated anger he had felt toward her and that he had spoken in a sharp manner.

After he returned from the license bureau, Daniel thumbed through the owner's manual. Inside he found a ten-dollar bill. He couldn't be certain, of course, but he suspected it was the same bill he had given Ogden and Jane earlier that day.

He arrived at Ogden and Jane's front door at ten o'clock the morning he and Jane had determined. Again, Jane answered the door promptly and Daniel found Ogden sitting in the same chair as he had occupied two days earlier.

"Well, Dr. Dan, the old doc said I'm holding my own, at least for now," he began in an animated, cheerful manner. "I believe they have finally regulated all those medications to a more livable dosage. I do know I'm feeling better than I did and I don't need any doctor to tell me that," he assured himself.

"That is good news. Glad to hear you are feeling better, O.R."

"Did you make a trip to the license bureau? Hope all went well there," Ogden inquired.

"That's all taken care of, O.R. You should have seen how those clerks reacted when they read the bill of sale and told me what I owed for sales tax. You can believe I gladly paid the seventy-cents for that fee!" he laughed as he sat in his usual chair and opened his notebook.

"O.R., I thank you and Jane for the car. Lucy asked me to extend her thanks, as well. She'll be calling Jane to express her personal thanks, I'm sure. By the way, I found a ten-dollar bill inside the owner's manual. Thought one of you might have hidden it there for a little emergency cash. Anyway," Daniel paused as he extended the bill toward Ogden, "here's your money."

"No, that's not our money," Ogden firmly stated as he waved Daniel's hand away. "You found it in your owner's manual, you say? It's your money. You tell Lucy we're pleased that you both can get good usage from the car. Both of you are very welcome.

"Now," Ogden clasped his hands and sat back, indicating he was prepared to move to a different topic of discussion, "We didn't talk very much about Tom Arthur when you were here the other day. Before I continue with what I want you to write, let me fill you in on old Tom. Since you and he will eventually have reason to work with each other, I think if you know a little of his background you'll be more comfortable when you need his assistance."

"Alright, Ogden. I would like to know a little about your old high school friend. As I said, I found Mr. Arthur to be a very different and interesting individual," he was pleased to allow Ogden to fulfill an obvious need to recall his relationship with a classmate who was now his attorney.

"Tom Arthur came from working-class people, just as I did," Ogden recalled, "his father and my father worked hourly, unskilled assembly jobs at RCA, down on Rogers Street. Tom was quite a character during his high school years, kind of a nice guy but not real sure of himself in many ways. As a result, he fell in with the wrong crowd during his junior year and became a member of a local Bloomington youth gang that called themselves 'The Black Aces.' Those guys weren't involved in anything serious compared to the gangs we have today. Oh sure, they would swipe cigarettes or candy from merchants, steal gasoline from any source readily available, and get into fights with anyone outside their group. Just usual, predictable mischief to prove they were rough and tough. Vandalism was a preferred activity they used to display their rebellious nature and bravado. Relatively petty infractions compared to today's criminality. Just being punks, you know.

"Back then, illegal drugs were practically unheard of in Bloomington. So, these fellows weren't really apprentice felons, as such, just kids who thought their anti-social behavior set them apart, gained them recognition because they were different... and tough!" Ogden smiled, paused and shifted himself to a different sitting position.

"Ogden, I heard of the Black Aces when I was in high school. I knew of a few tough dudes who claimed they were members, though I don't know if they were or not. I don't recall anything they ever did that made big news," he offered in agreement. "We had a few so-called 'hoods' at Smithburg High School. Those guys were a sight! They came to school wearing starched, ironed blue jeans, white tee shirts and shined, black wing-tipped dress shoes with as many metal caps on their shoe heels and toes as they could tack on. They seemed to prefer a very shiny, greasy hairstyle they called a 'd. a.' Do you remember that fancy hair style?" Daniel asked as he subdued his urge to laugh.

"That damned ridiculous d.a.," Ogden mused. "Sure, I remember that. All they needed to bring their self-degradation into the view of civilization was long, greased-up hair combed back, just so, to create what appeared to be a duck's ass perched on their heads. Oh yeah, the Aces were big on keeping their hair just so," he recalled as he chuckled with Daniel who now allowed himself a hearty laugh.

"With those shoes that were nailed up like a Clydesdale horse and their shiny hairdos, we could hear them coming down the hallway just before the shine from their hair would blind us if the sun was just right," Daniel continued his playful recollection. "Many of the girls, at least during my high school years, not to be outdone when it came

42

to hairstyle, fluffed and puffed their hair into what they called a bouffant. The white girls were unknowingly trying for the Afro-look long before the Afro came into style. Put one of those wanna-be hoods with his greased-up hair next to a bouffant girl and the sight was a laughable spectacle, as I remember. I must have gone through high school during an era of whacky hairdos!"

"Well," Ogden went on, "the boys in that crowd weren't angels, by anyone's definition. Sometimes they appeared comical, but they were never angelic. One night, long after all the stores closed and the streets were practically deserted, Tom and a few of his new friends were loafing around downtown Bloomington. As they walked south on College Avenue, one of them happened to notice a large plate-glass window across from where they had stopped to smoke, joke and... loaf. The topic of conversation quickly turned to daring each other to throw something through the window that had become the object of their attention. They didn't know who occupied the office and it wouldn't have made any difference to them if they had. That window, they decided, just had to be shattered," he paused to take a sip of coffee, then sat back and continued.

"After a few jousts and dares, Tom stepped forward to announce that if anybody could find a large enough rock or brick, he had the guts to do the job. Of course, one of them found Tom something to throw. Tom, not willing to back down from his bravado, as he was vying to become their undisputed leader, took the object, walked across the street and the window crashed into pieces.

"What Tom didn't know at the time was that he had broken the office window of a local attorney. The Bloomington police, naturally, were aware of Tom's gang. It wasn't long before various members of the Aces were called in for questioning. The attorney, mad as hell because he had to pay a large insurance deductible to have the window replaced, forced the issue. He demanded the police find out who had vandalized his property. He wanted payment, in full, for his loss. He refused to make a claim on his insurance policy because he planned to press the issue to his full satisfaction and not take one cent out of his pocket.

"It wasn't long," Ogden went on, "before one of the kids who witnessed the event, likely one of Tom's cheerleaders, confessed to the police he had watched as Tom shattered the window. Soon, an officer came to school and escorted old Tom to the police station.

"Tom didn't try to lie, make excuses or blame anyone for what he had done. The judge decided Tom would pay the lawyer for the damage he had caused, to the tune of five-hundred dollars, and, on top of that, there was a fine and court costs to be paid. The judge and prosecutor agreed Tom would avoid spending time in jail if he paid the fine and the damages he owed the lawyer.

Tom was barely able to scrape up enough money to pay the amount of the fine and court fees. He certainly didn't have five-hundred dollars to pay for the broken plate glass window. The prosecutor directed Tom to contact the lawyer to ask if he would agree to some sort of payment plan. If the wronged party wouldn't agree to some method of payment other than cash, the prosecutor cautioned, Tom should prepare to spend most of his summer months in the county jail. That's how Tom was unwittingly introduced to the legal profession," Ogden laughed.

"That lawyer wasn't about to back off from being compensated for his loss. Tom explained to him he wasn't able to pay cash for the damage he caused but he was willing to work until his debt was satisfied. Well," Ogden was obviously enjoying recalling his friend's youthful misconduct, "the lawyer owned farm land north of town out on Bottom Road. He told Tom he would allow him to work there, clearing fencerows, during the coming summer months when school wasn't in session. If that arrangement wasn't agreeable, the lawyer made his position very clear, or if Tom failed to fulfill his promise and complete the work to his specifications, the prosecutor would be notified.

"After a long, hot summer of hard labor without the possibility of earning any money for himself, Tom was out of the gang business. He completed high school, joined the Marine Corps for four years and then enrolled at Indiana University. Tom worked all the time he was in college, right on through law school. Tom Arthur is familiar with hard work, Dan," Ogden concluded.

"I sensed there was something different about him," Daniel stated. "He doesn't present an air of insincerity or try to come on as being superior to a happenstance visitor such as I was at our first meeting."

"That lawyer Tom worked for that summer?" Ogden returned to his subject, "allowed him to work in his office throughout the time Tom was a law student. They became close associates and even good friends. Second chances, Dan, we never know what can happen unless we allow and capitalize on a second chance," Ogden, seemingly saddened, became quiet as he contemplated what he had just said.

"Sure, a second chance," thought Daniel considering Ogden's discernable sadness. "How many of those have I wasted? I've sure been afforded several second chances but, unlike Thomas Arthur, I have not been smart enough or willing enough to use them to my advantage. Why would I think I deserve just one more chance? Ah, as Ogden said, 'Yesterday is dead and gone.' Yeah," Daniel recalled his yesterdays, "but if my past indicates anything about my future, I'll manage to achieve one more failure on my trail of disappointment," he concluded adding more fuel to a rising sense of disappointment with himself.

"O.R.," Daniel offered reviving himself from his negative thoughts while attempting to direct Ogden to the purpose of his visit and away from whatever had caused him to display sudden tiredness and a heavy visage, "you want to continue with where we left off last time I was here?"

"Okay, Dr. Dan, let's move on with that. Let's see. Refresh my memory. I believe we stopped when I arrived home with the bag in the trunk of my car. Is that right?" he asked as he redirected his thoughts and turned toward Daniel.

"Begin from there, orator Ogden, and I'll do my best to keep up as your scribe," Daniel added in an encouraging voice as he commanded his own demon to get behind him.

"When I got home that evening, as usual, I parked the car in the garage and went inside the house and mentioned to Jane what I had found. She wasn't overly concerned or alarmed about some article she assumed a student had discarded so we proceeded to have our evening meal. After we finished, I went out to the garage to examine the contents of the bag. Believe me," Ogden was now sitting almost ramrod straight in his chair, "I didn't expect to find anything like what was inside that bag!

"The bag was zippered, so I proceeded to slowly pull the closure open. At this stage, I admit, I was being cautious, as I had imagined everything from body parts to a dead alligator left there by some psycho. As I opened the bag, I soon discovered my dread and fear in that regard had been unfounded. There wasn't anything inside to cause bodily harm to whomever happened to have reason to explore those contents. What captured my attention was a musty smell. In an instant, I found myself staring at stacks of money bundled with rubber bands. Bundle stacked on bundle after bundle of money!" he stated emphatically.

"Leaving the satchel on the garage floor, I stepped back inside the house and told Jane what I had found in the bag. She followed me back to the garage to look for herself. She asked if I had found anything that might lead us to the owner. I explained that I had just opened the thing and hadn't looked that closely. We decided to move the money to the house to have a better look. There was not a thing inside the bag except… money. Just bundle after bundle of hundred, fifty, twenty and ten dollar bills, a few loose fives and ones. There was nothing else, not another scrap of anything, Dan…just money.

"Jane and I decided we should count the contents. I carried the satchel to the kitchen and we counted money for hours. When we finally finished, we sat staring at one another, amazed at the total figure. There was $1,444,881.00 stacked on our kitchen floor! When we realized who might have discarded such a huge amount of cash, we became worried. After all, would any legitimate organization tote around that much cash, then for any reason, carelessly discard or leave it in a gully? We couldn't imagine any legitimate organization being that careless with such a large amount of cash.

"Jane and I agreed we should put the money back inside the satchel and find a hiding place in the garage. We would wait until morning, which wasn't too long in coming, to decide how we would proceed.

Daniel didn't reply as he completed writing this latest revelation. When he had, finished the last sentence, he looked toward Ogden and thought, "Drug money! Ogden you had just cause to have been frightened. Those people don't call the police when they lose anything. Those people take care of their business themselves. They will go to any limit to protect *their* interests…and not bat an eye if that means murder." Daniel decided to keep those thoughts to himself. At this point, he didn't know how this story would end. Perhaps, once again, he was buying trouble by jumping to a wrong conclusion.

"Did you get all that down?" Ogden asked interrupting Daniel's silence.

"Yes, at least I am making progress. That was quite a find. My goodness…I never thought about anything like that…what did you and Jane decide to do?" He asked hoping for a reply that would calm his nerves and allay his fears.

"Just a minute," Ogden replied as he turned slightly in his chair and called out to his wife who was nearby in the kitchen, "Jane, isn't it about time for my midday medicine?"

With that, Jane came into the room with a glass of water and a capsule. "Yes dear, it's time. Are you beginning to feel uncomfortable?" she asked as she handed him the medication and exchanged the glass of water for his coffee cup.

"According to the way I'm beginning to feel, it must be long past the time, let's put it that way," Ogden said, then sat back in a relaxed position after he had sipped enough water to accommodate the large capsule.

"Do you think it would be better if I came back tomorrow," Daniel volunteered as he noticed Ogden shifting himself, almost struggling for a less painful position.

"Dan," Jane volunteered, "I think tomorrow would be better. Ogden tires easily and after he takes his medication, he usually sleeps for an hour or two. Is that alright with you?" Jane asked as she looked toward Ogden seeking his consent.

"I believe I've had it for today. The medicine works fast but it doesn't work for long. Right now, I need a little rest and a break from sitting in this chair. Hope you understand. Come back tomorrow and we'll continue…there's more I need to tell you, but it will have to wait," Ogden finished as he closed his eyes as the powerful drug began to mask his pain.

After Daniel departed, Jane returned to where Ogden was now half-sitting, half-slumping in his chair, carrying a walker. "Let me help you get to the bedroom, dear," Jane offered. "You can rest better in there. When you wake up, I'll fix you something to eat. Whatever sounds good to you, okay?" she offered in a soothing voice as she assisted him to an upright sitting position.

"What would I do without you?" Ogden stated as Jane helped him to stand up and grasp the walker. "Thanks for not bringing this thing," he nodded toward the contrivance that had become a necessary aid, "in the room while Dan was here. He doesn't need to know how weak and dependent I've become."

"Right now, it's our little secret, Ogden," Jane teased as she steadied him as he inched his way through the hallway and into their bedroom.

"Jane," Ogden began, as he lowered himself to the bed, "sometimes I wonder how much longer I can will myself to hang on. When the painkiller wears off, I'm brought back to reality and any thought of surviving this thing much longer becomes hard for me to imagine. Sometimes I wish I could just slip away and not be a burden to you," he slurred.

"There, there, my sweetheart. You stretch out and rest now. Remember, medical science does work miracles. We have each other and we still have hope, don't we?" Jane asked, seeking to reassure herself as she stroked his arm and kissed his cheek.

Ogden stared piercingly into Jane's eyes as the strong narcotic rushed through his system clouding his mind and disabling his ability and will to reply. "Sleep now, my darling Ogden," Jane whispered as she pulled a coverlet up to cover his shoulders. She quietly stepped from the room wiping tears of hurt and sadness from her eyes.

CHAPTER 12

Jane met Ogden over forty years earlier while she was working in her parent's shoe store in downtown Fayetteville, North Carolina. Ogden was serving at nearby Ft. Bragg and had ventured into town one Saturday afternoon to buy a pair of civilian dress shoes. Jane just happened to be the person who greeted him when he entered the store.

During the course of finding shoes to Ogden's liking, Jane began to notice how different Ogden appeared to the usual military clientele that shopped their store. Ogden wasn't brash, loud or discourteous but an obviously kind and considerate man. "Even at three o'clock on a Saturday afternoon, he didn't reek of beer or strong drink," Jane noticed. "He was by himself, which, I would learn, was true to Ogden's nature. In many ways, to this day, he prefers to be by himself. Perhaps," she thought as she assisted him during that first meeting, "this very handsome young man may warrant my further consideration and interest."

Ogden paid cash for his shoes and she didn't see him again for almost three weeks. On the third Saturday after his first visit to the store, Ogden returned feigning interest in buying yet another pair of shoes. He declined assistance from another employee, continuing to shop and stall as he browsed one pair and then another, until Jane was free so he could ask her a question, any question, to draw her attention to him. When she finally walked toward Ogden, he quickly returned the shoe he had been eyeing back on the display rack. "Back again for another pair of shoes so soon?" she asked, with a smile that conveyed her pleasure in seeing him.

"Do you have this style in any color other than black?" Ogden stammered aloud, as his eyes focused on the very beautiful young woman who was standing close by his side, making him forget about the shoe he had been holding as his mouth suddenly felt very dry.

"Well, let's see. If I remember correctly, you need a size ten, regular width. I believe we have that style in brown and cordovan, but... now, honestly, did you really come here today to buy another pair of dress shoes or is there something else that might have brought you back to our store?" Jane smiled and asked quizzically offering Ogden opportunity to relax and state what was on his mind.

"Well, yes... there is something else I had thought about...wanted to... ask you," Ogden gaining some encouragement by Jane's playful question and inviting smile, stammered. "Would you be interested in going out... to dinner tonight? I mean, that is, dinner with me? That is... if you aren't already busy with something else or somebody else...or if you just don't want to...I'll understand. But, yes, you're right, I don't really need another pair of shoes right now, that is, not at least more dress shoes..." Ogden felt he couldn't stop talking, saying anything at this stage, as he feared Jane would probably laugh him out of the store if he stopped talking and waited for her reply.

"Will you be wearing the new shoes you bought from me a few weeks ago?" Jane asked, still smiling, as she placed yet another shoe Ogden had nervously grabbed back in its proper location on the display rack "Thank you. Yes, I would like to go to dinner with you this evening. You choose the place. I'll leave work around five. I live with my parents at 605 East Sycamore. You can stop by there, say, around seven?" Jane replied answering Ogden's question and providing information Ogden would likely forget to ask considering how unnerved he seemed at the prospect of asking her for a date.

Jane and Ogden dated for almost a year before they married. They lived near Ft. Bragg for four months before the Army transferred him to Ft. Benning, Georgia. From there, Ogden deployed to Vietnam and Jane moved back to Fayetteville to be near her parents. All through Ogden's years of military service, Jane was the supportive military spouse. After all, she was accustomed to the transitory life-style of the service family. Her father had retired from the Army ten years before she and Ogden met.

In 1967, Ogden returned from his last tour of duty overseas. Due to his wounded lower left leg and ankle, he spent the next six months at Walter Reed Army Hospital with Jane remaining close at his side. After two corrective surgeries and rehabilitation were completed, Ogden was rated disabled and honorably discharged from the Army. With his military career brought to a premature close, Ogden and Jane re-located to Bloomington, Indiana.

Jane, with experience in the retail business, eventually purchased and operated a women's apparel shop. The store had become available at an attractive price due to low sales traffic in a downtown area suffering from strip mall expansions all around the city. Though a financial struggle during the earlier years, the store became a profitable enterprise as the downtown area underwent revitalization. "Jane's" eventually became the shop of choice for women who preferred expert customer service and fine clothing. As Ogden's illness advanced and he required increasing care, Jane sold the business in order to be readily available to assist her husband.

Ogden's war disability precluded him from working jobs that required standing for a prolonged time. While he exercised diligently to maintain his superior upper body strength, his weakened leg limited his capacity to stand or bend throughout a normal workday. Of all the possible civilian occupations he had considered while on active military duty, a career in sales of any kind had never crossed his mind. Ogden wasn't a glad-hander or the life of any party. After investigating other pursuits, he determined a career as an insurance sales representative might be a good fit for him. If honesty, hard work and thoroughness were valued traits in the insurance industry, he had written on his job application form, he felt assured he would become a successful agent.

Ogden Royal had been away for almost fourteen years by the time they moved back to his hometown. Both his parents had long since passed away. His father had died suddenly before Ogden completed high school. His mother died from injuries sustained in an automobile accident in 1956. After that tragic event, Ogden, as an only child, didn't have family or any other reason that compelled him to re-visit his childhood home.

While former friends and acquaintances weren't aware of Ogden's heroic military service, many remembered his name and his success as a high school wrestler. One of Ogden's classmates offered to help him find employment and steered him toward the insurance agency where he would meet Daniel in 1978.

Ogden and Jane eventually bought a house after both settled into their new careers. Their first home was located south of town, on Rockport Road. Their second home, the house Daniel would visit, was west of Bloomington, on North Maple Grove Road. While the first house was modest, their current residence, situated on five acres, was spacious and had been custom-built. Ogden and Jane had purchased this property in 1996, as Daniel would eventually learn.

CHAPTER 13

The high school Daniel attended, eventually closed by the contagion and lure of consolidation, was in the same county as Bloomington but had little in common with that international community. Most Smithburg teachers lived in Bloomington and hurriedly evacuated that rural community each day before the last school bus was off the premises. Those teachers were not seeking permanent employment at such a remote high school. As itinerants, they had signed on just long enough for their spouse, or themselves, to complete an advanced degree at Indiana University. All too often, they remained on the faculty for a year or two before departing for a better opportunity. Those young teachers weren't stakeholders in the community and they nimbly avoided the bother they supposed would follow if they became involved with the welfare of their students. As a result, the quality of secondary education offered by temporary teachers was generally ineffective.

Many students who might have succeeded under the guidance of caring teachers faced failure once they ventured outside the walls of that school. Most graduates were simply not prepared to pursue higher education due to the negligence by those so-called professionals who taught only for a paycheck. As a result, few of those abused students were motivated or determined to risk pursuing education or training beyond high school. Daniel, sensing an inward need to improve his station in life, and encouraged by his parents, decided he would become one of the few.

His first experience with higher education was at a small private college in Minnesota where he enrolled after graduation from high school. Daniel didn't actually choose that particular school but, rather, had been recruited by the school's basketball coach. Upon an offer of paid tuition, an opportunity to play basketball and to delay working a low-paying, unskilled job for the rest of his life, he eagerly accepted the coach's offer. For the first time in his life, he began to develop an interest in schoolwork. As a result, he would look back with fond memories of the time he spent at that school. While he didn't make or maintain a friendship with many students, he had kept casual contact with one acquaintance who became a medical doctor.

As his first year ended, Daniel began to make plans to transfer to Indiana University whose campus was just a few miles from his parent's home. He came to regard that choice as one of several bad decisions he would make.

While a student at the large university, Daniel enrolled in the Army Reserve Officers Training Corps. His father had served over five years, as an enlistee, from early 1940 to the end of the European war. Daniel, out of admiration for that brave soldier, decided service to his country would become part of his experience. After graduation, Daniel reported to Ft. Benning, Georgia to begin his active duty service. His next duty assignment was at Ft. Polk, then back to Ft. Benning for additional training. He qualified and became accepted to the Jungle Warfare School, taught by Army combat veterans and CIA agents, Ft. Sherman, Panama, Canal Zone before deployment to serve a year as a junior infantry officer in Vietnam. One of his battalion commanders had spoken with Daniel several times to encourage him to stay in the Army and make that his career. Feeling fortunate to have survived a non-life threatening wound, he felt one year in that region fulfilled his obligation. He wasn't about to commit to repeating that experience.

Once separated from the Army, Daniel enrolled to complete an advanced degree at Indiana University. From there, he had taught public school for five years and was tenured, meaning he had achieved the sixth school-year contract that offered job security for as long as he chose to teach, barring misconduct or insubordination. Again, feeling dissatisfied and that he had more to prove to himself, he resigned his position. Teaching, though he believed students had enjoyed his classes and held him in high regard, hadn't held his interest and he wanted to earn more money for his new wife and growing family.

Daniel soon regretted he had abandoned a secure teaching position for a highly competitive job as an insurance sales representative. Whatever had been the perceived positive factors that had attracted him to that career choice didn't overcome the reality of longer hours and little time away from work and an income dependent on the whims and preferences of other people. While never unemployed or reprimanded for poor performance, he became dissatisfied and jumped from one company to another always hoping the next position would bring satisfaction. His quest remained unfulfilled until, out of despair, he left the insurance business for a position as a manager at a franchised auto dealership. Again, that position required long hours but the compensation was over double of any income he had previously earned. That would be his last fulltime job before he reached retirement age.

He had realized, by accident, what he should have been doing with his life long before he left the auto dealership. As an avid reader and amateur writer, he had composed articles and submitted them for publication in periodicals and newspapers. When the local newspaper advertised for columnists, he submitted a few examples of his work to the editor. He knew the competition would be stiff as Bloomington is an enclave of frustrated artists of all genres. He may have been a malcontent concerning his occupation but never shied away from an appealing challenge. When the editor from the newspaper called to say he had been selected as a columnist, he didn't attempt to hide his surprise or elation. He soon began to feel he was not working for the paper but rather he was finally performing a labor of love.

For the first time since his early days in the military, he was doing something he deemed challenging and rewarding. He enjoyed the lonely endeavor of sitting in front of the computer terminal to assemble his thoughts in a public format available to an unknown reading public. As a writer, he looked forward to hearing from readers whether they agreed or disagreed with his thoughts.

Before he and Ogden met that October morning at Smitty's to re-establish a waning relationship, he had finished publishing his first book. As he told Lucy, he wasn't concerned with the number of books that would be sold, he intended to fulfill an objective he promised himself he would attain. He soon learned writing a saleable book entails a particular set of skills and required intensity and discipline. He proved to himself he was up to those tasks. Marketing the work, however, brought him to realize his lack of training and unfamiliarity with the publishing industry presented obstacles he was not able to overcome. Sales, or more specifically the lack of sales, contrary to what he had told himself and his wife, did matter. If nothing else, he often reminded himself, working with Ogden might offer one last opportunity to accomplish something that would prove truly meaningful.

CHAPTER 14

The following day Daniel returned anxious to continue the account Ogden had introduced before becoming weary and uncomfortable. As he entered the room he had left just a few hours earlier, he found his friend seated in his usual chair. He noticed Ogden did not offer a greeting or acknowledge his presence in a welcoming manner as he walked across the room. As he quietly seated himself, he noticed Ogden was awake; at least his eyes were open, but he remained motionless with his gaze fixed on the opposite wall. Though neatly dressed, Ogden appeared pale and much weaker than he had the day before. He decided to risk breaking an awkward silence by asking, "How are you this morning, O.R.?" as he feigned interest in organizing his notebook.

"I...uh, I rested pretty well for most of last night, but I'm not going to win any endurance contest this morning," Ogden, seemingly jolted into awareness, replied in a terse voice void of emotion while he slowly lifted his head and looked toward Daniel.

"Before I interrupted you, you seemed to be resting. I apologize if I bothered you," he volunteered as he noticed Ogden's apparent need to shift himself to a less confining position.

"No, no. Don't apologize. There's nothing you need to apologize to me for. The medication is kicking in so we can get on with it. When you came in, I wasn't asleep, just deep in thought. Isn't it amazing how thinking about something else occupies the mind and eliminates other problems, at least for a short time?"

"Mind over matter, O.R.?"

"Call it whatever you like, but thoughts are powerful, for good or evil, depending on how they are used."

"Ogden, I'll stay as long as you are comfortable. When you feel you have talked enough, just say the word and I'll move along," he offered with a faint smile hoping to counteract a heavy mood he sensed might impede or preclude their conversation. As he had spoken, he studied Ogden's eyes for those unmistakable signs his illness had progressed to the point where a rapid decline of physical capacity and mental alertness were eminent.

"Okay," Ogden began, appearing somewhat revived, "where did we leave off yesterday? Oh yes. Jane and I counted the money and found a hiding place in the garage. We had decided to wait until the next morning to decide the best course of action. Is that right?" he summarized with surprising speed and accuracy, as he seemed to regain vigor and a more welcoming visage as he pulled himself to an alert position.

"Take it from there, Ogden. I'm all ears to learn more about what you did next. Wow! What a lump of jack to deal with. Go ahead, I don't want to slow you down with my commentary," he stated while directing his focus toward Ogden.

"The morning," Ogden started, "couldn't come fast enough to suit me. I didn't sleep much or rest the entire few hours after we counted the money. My mind raced until I gave up on sleep, so I was up early agonizing over what to do next. Of course, Jane was concerned so we sat down and re-hashed what had transpired. I remember telling her I didn't think, but wasn't absolutely sure, there had been anyone around who had noticed me loading the bag into the trunk of my car. The more I thought about that possibility, the more concerned I became. After all," he paused, "what if someone had been lurking underneath the west side stadium stands watching me load the bag? What if someone had been standing guard to make sure the right person came to retrieve the money? I began to play what if games in my mind," he stated as he leaned back for a drink of coffee while Daniel struggled to keep his notes current.

"We decided to wait for a few days to see if anything came out in the local or Indianapolis newspapers concerning the whereabouts of such a large amount of money," he continued. "If any legitimate business was involved, no matter how irresponsible they had been with caring for such a large asset, we thought there would be some public notice. If, on the other hand, this money belonged to an illegal organization, the owners would not be going to the authorities or to the media. We decided not do anything, say anything to anyone, until we assured ourselves the money did not belong to a legitimate concern," he paused as Daniel continued writing.

"I'm about caught up now, if you want to continue," Daniel stated as he hurriedly wrote what he had been told and looked up from his notes, indicating he was ready to proceed.

"We waited for two weeks without hearing or reading anything about the money from any news source. At that time, we had other questions we needed to answer and other decisions to make. As I said before, the money, though neatly bound in various denominations, had a particular, strong odor. I decided to unzip the satchel, stack the money on a blanket in the garage to expose that muskiness to a good airing. At the same time, I examined the bills to see if I could detect any markings that might indicate the money came from a bank. The money, though not crisp and new, was not marked in any way I could detect. The condition of the bills tended to reassure Jane and me the money didn't belong to any legitimate concern. We decided I had accidentally come up on a stash left there, for whatever reason or purpose, by an illegal drug ring. If that was the case, I had to be sure I hadn't been seen by anyone as I drove away from the stadium," he emphasized by a pause he employed to take a quick sip of coffee.

"A few more days passed with the money still spread out on the garage floor, he continued. "We hadn't discussed carrying any of that loot with us and hadn't thought of spending even one dollar. About that time, I did decide I should trade cars," Ogden explained, "because if I had been seen, that white Buick I drove at that time would be noticeable and could easily be traced back to me. While I hadn't planned on a different vehicle, I thought it was a necessary precaution. Of course, I didn't want my old car sitting on a local car lot, so one afternoon I drove down to Bedford intending to trade it for something different.

"I drove around town and eventually visited a dealership located on Seventh Street. I soon decided Bedford wasn't quite far enough away from Bloomington, so I drove south through Mitchell then on to the small town of Salem. I figured my old car wasn't likely to be noticed or connected with me from a remote car lot nearly sixty miles from home. I had become fixated, I suppose, on the thought someone might have watched as I lifted the bag into the trunk of my car.

"At the dealership in Salem, I met a likeable young man who seemed agreeable and anxious to make a sale. After a test drive or two, we came to terms on a price difference and he directed me to another fellow to complete the sale transaction. After exchanging pleasantries, that fellow took my credit application and completed the appropriate paperwork.

"All the time I was applying for credit, I was thinking about all that cash lying on our garage floor. To make a long story short, I drove back home in a different car. No sense, I thought, in driving a car around home that had any possibility of being recognized by someone, unseen by me, lurking about as I left the stadium that evening a few weeks earlier," he paused once again to allow Daniel time to record his words.

"Once the car situation was resolved to my satisfaction," Ogden pressed on, "we had other worries to deal with. Dan…" Ogden looked up fixing his stare on his scribe, "Jane and I never discussed going to the police about finding the money. For whatever reason, moral or otherwise, we agreed the money was ours unless something broke in the news to change our minds. We waited and watched for another two months and didn't hear or see a word about it anywhere. We began to consider how we could quietly begin to launder that cash and get it into our accounts. We knew we had to avoid moving a large amount of money at one swoop. As you know, any cash transaction of ten-thousand dollars or more requires federal paperwork. We didn't want to raise eyebrows, mind you, and at this early stage, we were still hesitant to spend even a dollar of the money," he explained as he turned his attention toward the kitchen and called, "Jane, can you come in for a few minutes? Will you please tell Dan how we began to filter cash from the bag into our accounts?" Ogden addressed his wife in a gentle manner.

"Sure, you take a break, Ogden," Jane replied as she entered the room and sat down. "I know this part of our circuitous financial workings. I'm ready when you are," Jane paused as Daniel struggled to complete Ogden's words.

"Okay, I'm caught up. Go ahead when you're ready," Daniel answered.

"Well," she began, "I was operating the women's clothing store, as you know. Most people, even back then, paid with a credit card. A few, however, were true cash customers. It wasn't uncommon, on top of credit card receipts, for me to end up an average day with between five-hundred and a thousand dollars of cash in the drawer. We hadn't used a single dollar of the money up to that time. To be honest, we were afraid to circulate the money for fear it had been marked in some manner we couldn't determine. So, we decided I should take a few of the bills from the bag with me each day to work. At the end of the day, I would trade money. Maybe a twenty-dollar bill at first, just to see if that generated any unwelcome attention. If the bank had shown any alarm concerning my deposit, I would explain the bill came in from an unknown cash transaction. We planned to increase the volume of exchange as we gained confidence," Jane explained without emotion.

"The first bill I deposited was accepted and credited without being questioned or flagged by the bank, so I waited a day or two and exchanged two bills. From there out, I would exchange more and more money and eventually began to trade the larger bills from my cash drawer. It wasn't long before I was trading almost all the cash paid by customers for the money Ogden found. We never had any problem with our laundering scheme, I suppose it should be called," she smiled.

"Even with our successful exchange program going full force, we still had a problem," she continued. "Some days I would bring home more than a thousand dollars in cash I had swapped out of the store drawer. Now the question became how to filter all that 'clean' cash into our personal accounts. You can't walk into a bank lobby, day after day, with a substantial amount of cash to deposit in a personal account without drawing attention. We decided we had to keep a low profile. We didn't go out and buy anything flashy or flaunt our sudden wealth. We didn't actually spend any of the money until we decided to begin paying for everyday purchases by using cash. A little at a time, you know," Jane paused watching Daniel as he continued to record her words.

"All the time," Ogden added, "Jane and I kept an ear to the ground for any hint concerning the origin of that bag of cash. By this time, we began to gain confidence that all was well on that score. We were concerned mind you, but becoming more confident as time wore on. We hadn't made much of a dent in the contents of that bag, but we didn't really have to be in a hurry. When I went to the bank with my paycheck, I would deposit almost the entire amount while taking very little cash. After all, I had access to plenty of cash. That way, we would be able to transfer money to other accounts without drawing undue attention to our little operation," Ogden concluded.

"We weren't making much progress with all that money," Jane interjected. "Ogden decided to contact his old friend, Tom Arthur, to ask him for his advice without going into the details we are now sharing with you. For all Tom knew, or even knows to this day, we had saved and accumulated a substantial amount of cash. The source was immaterial to him and he didn't ask prying questions. All he needed to know was that we had money we wanted to move offshore for tax and privacy purposes. Tom did some searching and introduced us to a banker located in Antigua. To say the least, our deposit with that bank that eventually exceeded a million dollars is now worth, according to the last statement, well over three million. That banker may not be on the absolute level, but he has done an excellent job with the money. Dan, we could pay back that $1,444.881, with legal interest, and net a small fortune, if that should ever become necessary," she surmised.

"We have this house, a cabin near Grand Marais, Minnesota located on Mayhew Lake, a few rental units, our brokerage and savings accounts, and our vehicles on top of that," Ogden continued. "We didn't waste anything. I'd say we could show an additional two-million, not counting what life insurance we both own, if we liquidated, on top of the offshore amount Jane just mentioned. We are sure the money I found came from ill-gotten methods. We want some of our good fortune used to help those who need and deserve help. We'll talk more about that later. Before we go into that, there is more to our story I want to tell you…but not this morning. I've reached my limit and it's time for my medication, isn't it dear?" he said as he turned toward Jane.

"Yes it is," as she glanced at her wristwatch, "and I can see you are tiring. Dan, maybe you will come back tomorrow? Ogden, I can tell, is growing uncomfortable and needs to rest," she stated, heralding the conclusion of that meeting.

"Give me a few seconds to finish my notes and I'll get out of here and plan to see you both tomorrow," Daniel agreed as he finished his writing for the day. With that, he bid them both a good day and departed with his mind fuller and busier than his notebook.

"These people are worth over five million dollars," Daniel thought as he drove the few miles back to his home. "No wonder," he studied, "they didn't think twice about giving away a car worth thirty-thousand dollars. Just a drop in the bucket to them, I suppose," as he continued his mental gymnastics. "What was it Ogden meant when he stated, *'We want some of our good fortune used to help those who need and deserve help,'*" he asked himself. "Perhaps that is that 'second part' he mentioned when he first discussed this matter with me back at Smitty's," his mind continued to race. "Ogden and Jane may be planning for me to help them straighten this matter out and eventually disburse their fortune to various groups who merit financial assistance. I wonder how much Tom Arthur knows about all this," he tired himself with runaway speculation.

Once their welcomed visitor had departed their home, Jane helped Ogden to their bedroom where he would sleep, she hoped, for the next two or three hours. As she helped him to a comfortable lying position, she asked, "Ogden, how much more do you intend to tell him? Are you planning to tell him about that scary creep who called the dress shop and threatened me?" As he stared wearily at Jane and attempted to stammer a reply, the powerful medication drew him into a deep sleep.

CHAPTER 15

Ogden had learned to trust his senses and reflexes as he trained to become a champion high school wrestler and later as an Army combatant. That evening at Memorial Stadium as he loaded the money-laden satchel into the trunk of his car, he had a feeling, an unexplainable sensation somebody was watching him. The untrained and less wary often detect an undecipherable feeling of discomfort when they sense unseen eyes of the silent and secretive are upon their person. Ogden had learned to follow his innate, primal nature and as a result, had survived where others, less honed and instinctual, had been defeated or died.

As time passed without incident, he began to console himself and his nagging suspicion began to subside. Whatever it was he had apparently misread as a cause for wariness, he began to consider as groundless. Billy Merritt, by mere coincidence, would soon step out of his dark world and reaffirm to Ogden that he should not have second-guessed his senses to detect those lying in ambush.

Family lore held that Billy's great-great grandfather settled and owned a large tract of land that now includes present-day Cocoa Beach, Florida. Merritt Island, now the location of the Kennedy Space Center and nearly 36,000 permanent residents, as earlier Merritt generations had proudly recounted their family history, supposedly bears the name of that early settler. That facet of family history, perhaps partly true or a total fabrication was not interesting or important as far as Billy was concerned. When Billy's grandfather moved his family to Indiana, that branch of the family soon fell onto hard times and eventually into disgrace. While the Merritt family was once, long ago, accomplished and honorable, Billy's father became the town lay-about and drunkard. Billy never concerned himself with issues of family pride, honor or personal morality. Those matters were as foreign and inconsequential to him as his family history.

Billy was a Bloomington street tough who lived with his mother but habitually slept and ate wherever he could find shelter and a free meal. He had barely graduated from high school in 1972. Sometime toward the end of his junior year, he began fantasizing and bragging that, right after he graduated, he would join the Marine Corps. In order to fulfill his bravado, although he suffered frequent and gnawing second thoughts, he joined the Corps before the end of his senior year. Three weeks after his high school graduation, he found himself in boot camp at Parris Island, South Carolina.

Boot camp, to his eye-popping surprise, was nothing near what Billy had expected. He hadn't realized that wanting something and attaining that same goal often require paying a price, demanding a discipline, the casual braggart finds beyond his fortitude. He rankled toward the strong males that comprised the cadre of drill sergeants. Billy soon became a problematic "boot" and earned himself the title of "Numbnuts" by his Marine drill instructor. Because of repeated unacceptable performance and a penchant to have the last word, he found himself on the re-cycle list and had to repeat boot camp. Before Billy earned the honor of becoming a "Marine," he earned a reputation of being a troublemaker by those who had experienced the displeasure of his presence.

Due to malingering, insubordination and conduct unbecoming a Marine, Billy was discharged from the Corps after serving less than one full year. He became one of the "few" recruits deemed unfit to wear the uniform of the "proud." Throughout the remainder of his life, the designation of "undesirable" led Billy "Numbnuts" Merritt to failure followed by failure.

Soon after he returned to Bloomington under a cloud of self-imposed dishonor, he happened to peruse an old magazine that featured a story about Richard Speck. Speck, an amoral psychopath, had murdered eight student nurses as they slept in their South Chicago apartment July 14, 1966. The prose that recounted the acts of a lunatic didn't interest Billy as his reading ability and comprehension was marginal at best. What did capture his attention was the image of Speck's tattoo, that read, "Born to Raise Hell." "If someone as famous as this guy thinks that's cool, then it's cool enough for me," he thought.

A few days later, Billy called upon the only tattoo artist then in town. When told the preferred message would cost him twenty-five dollars, he began to negotiate. "Hey, what can I get for fifteen bucks? That's all the money I have on me," Billy asked becoming nervous and impatient. In reality, he didn't have a dollar he had actually earned himself. Resorting to his tried and true method of obtaining money, Billy had cajoled his work-weary mother for yet another "loan" that he didn't have means or intention to re-pay.

"Well, I could do a small, one-color three-word tat for fifteen dollars," offered the artist. "How about something like, 'Born to Lose,' that's a catchy statement I've done before," he enthusiastically concluded as he needed the money and didn't want to risk arousing Billy's notable wrath.

"Okay, go ahead with that. Put it right here," Billy said indicating his right forearm, closer to his wrist than to his elbow.

Billy sat very still as the semi-illiterate tattoo artist carved a very black and ungrammatical scar on his arm that blazoned, "Born To Loose." Billy, from that time forward, unknowingly and involuntarily announced his comical stupidity to those he met without the necessity of uttering a word.

Ogden stopped by Jane's shop one early-August morning to ask if she was available for lunch. They often escaped from their daily occupations for a coffee break or a sandwich at Jane's favorite restaurant, Nick's Olde English Hut, located three blocks from the center of downtown. "Not today, Ogden," she replied. "I'm short one employee so I'll have to stay here. Would you mind going to Nick's and bring sandwiches back here? We can go in the backroom for a short lunch break, if you want to do that," she offered as she arranged a new inventory of blouses on a rack.

"That sounds good to me. I'll be back just as soon as the sandwiches are ready. Hey," he stopped short of the door and turned, "why don't you call down there now and place our order? That should save a few minutes waiting around and allow me a little more time to be with my favorite gal," he smiled as Jane began walking toward the telephone.

Ogden decided he would drive the short distance to the restaurant as his crippled left leg had been acting arthritic due, he assumed, to the humid weather common during that time of year. Kirkwood Avenue, where Nick's was located, was always crowded and busy so after a hectic search, he found a parking spot in a lot on Fourth Street and walked the short distance to the restaurant.

Billy was seated at a table by a window inside McDonald's with Tucker Warren, a homeless kick-about during those brief interludes when he wasn't confined to the county lock-up for being drunk, drugged or vagrant. Tucker, due to his on-going use of methamphetamine, often displayed the early signs of aphasia or, during his better days, a very short attention span.

"Tuck," Billy began becoming excited, "do you see that gimp-ass who just now walked across the street goin' into Nick's?"

"Yeah, so what about 'im," Tucker replied while feigning interest as he gummed, then managed to find the side of his mouth where he still had a few teeth, then choked down a half-eaten, discarded hamburger he had fished out of the trash can while the counter attendant was distracted by a paying customer. "Just wish we'd a got here before they quit servin' breakfas. One of them egg muffins sure would have been tasty," Tucker grumbled, unthankful for his good fortune or to the person who had unintentionally given him a discarded sandwich he had just enjoyed as his free lunch.

"I remember seein' that guy somewhere," Billy stated ignoring Tucker's inattention and lack of concern, "Yeah, that's the limp, that gimp, I've seen… somewhere before. I've seen that leg-dragger someplace but I can't place him right now," he mused, as his eyes remained fixated on the front door of Nick's that Ogden had just entered.

"You think he may have a few bucks we could rip off?" Tucker beamed with interest as he thought of the meth he could score if he came into some quick, easy money. "Don't look like he would be too tough to hammer, if that's what you're thinkin.' We could wait for him to leave, follow him and do our thing. What are you thinkin' now, Numbnuts? Wanna put the punch on 'im?" Tucker asked, suddenly riveted on what Billy was saying as he ruminated on the possibility of a drug-induced high that never failed to rivet his thinking and lead him to become carelessly mouthy.

"What did you call me, Tuck? Huh? I've told you not to call me that name, you bastard. Just because I told you, when I was a little drunk, what those asshole Marine jackasses called me doesn't mean I want everyone around here remindin' me of it. Got it, Tuck? Let that slip again and I'll knock a few more of your rotted front teeth out," raged Billy loud enough that customers standing at the counter turned their attention toward the two slovenly men seated by the window.

"Okay, okay. It just slipped, Bill. It won't happen again. Cool down. I didn't mean to call you that," Tucker stammered a quick apology. "What are you thinkin' about that wimpy-looking guy? Think we should take him?" Tucker offered hoping to steer Billy's attention toward a mutually profitable plan that might forestall a beating that was almost certain to follow his careless slip of the tongue.

"For sure, you are a sorry ass," Billy hissed in a more subdued voice. "Now shut up while I think. Don't know yet, so cool your heels, Tuck," he continued calmly and firmly as he struggled to regain what little determination he could muster to control his explosive emotions. "No doubt in my military mind we could deck that gimp-ass and take whatever money he has on 'em. That ain't what's on my mind right now, Tuck. As I said, I've seen that guy someplace that I can't remember right now. Let me do some thinkin' and see if I can recall where that might have been. Nah, we can't rob the gimp right here during daylight anyways. Use your dumb-assed, drug-soaked head for once. Sometimes I don't know why I allow you to hang around anywhere near me," Billy concluded becoming more menacing as he watched Ogden walk back across Kirkwood headed south to where he had parked his car.

When Billy and Tucker decided not to follow Ogden Royal and attempt to rob him, they unknowingly made the best decision they would make that day. Within their world of instant gratification, where they didn't have much reason to respect themselves, they were devoid of being capable of respecting another human being. Billy had not been listening when his Marine instructors emphasized the danger of underestimating the enemy.

Later that afternoon, Tucker meekly turned to Billy and asked through a freshly split lip, "Where you sleepin' tonight, Bill? Thought I'd make my way over to the football stadium and sleep underneath the west stands. Lookin' like rain this evening, so that might be the best and driest place for us, that is, if you ain't plannin' to head for your mom's place. What do you think about that?"

"Tuck, you can be a real clever bastard sometimes! For sure, you are usually clueless, usually muddle-headed, but once in a great while you stumble into somethin' that matters. That's where I saw that gimp! You know, the guy we saw limpin' his ass across Kirkwood when we were moochin' at McDonald's? Yeah, that's it! That guy was out there one evening crip-assin' around the stadium when I was comin' off a drunk, hangin' out underneath the stands gettin' ready to bed down."

"Yeah, well, so what? Is that why you didn't want to kick his ass and take his money?"

"No...hell no! Listen to me. Right before he left that night, he drove his car around to the west side and messed around with a gym bag, or somethin' he found in a ditch. After he gazed around to see if anybody was watchin' him, he loaded the bag into the trunk of his car. That's where I saw him before, Tuck! Wonder what in hell was in that bag?" Billy mused while staring at Tucker who gazed vacuously at Billy as he slowly tried to discern how and why he ever been "clever."

After a few days passed, Billy recalled hearing of a botched money drop that supposedly took place somewhere in Bloomington by one of the drug running rings from Detroit. "I'll bet I know who got their money," he thought. "Never heard anything about the money bein' found by anyone. Hells bells," Billy exclaimed to himself, now excited by the possibilities he was beginning to envision, "I'll bet the gimp got their money! That's what he was loadin' that evening there at the football stadium."

A week or so after his labored and fortuitous recollection, Billy found Tucker hanging around People's Park in his usual half-drugged condition. "Hey, Tuck, come over here and clear your faded meth-head for a minute. Sit down, shut up and listen to me 'cause we gotta talk."

"Yeah, I'm a little faded alright, what's it to ya? Talk? Whatta 'bout," Tucker replied slowly as he shuffled toward Billy with glistening eyes and a ragged-tooth, spacey grimace that readily confirmed his addiction to methamphetamine was exacting a heavy toll on both his body and mind.

"About the gimp you wanted to rob that day when we were sittin' over there," Billy replied pointing across the street toward the fast-food restaurant. "Remember that guy? We need to find out a little more about that little man, Tuck."

"I don't know who the hell he is, but I know where he works, Billy-boy, Billy-boy," Tucker answered in a singsong rhythm as he flashed an all-knowing, nearly toothless grin.

"Okay, smart-ass. Sit down and take that stupid grin off your rotten-toothed face," Billy replied as he grabbed Tucker's arm and assisted him onto the bench. "Where's he work?"

"He, my good friend Billy Numbnuts Merritt, works in a freakin' dress shop downtown on College just across from the damned courthouse," Tucker finished just as Billy punched him in the mouth that instantaneously removed all remnants of what had been a self-assured smile.

"Dress shop? The gimp works in a dress shop? Come on, Tuck, get your dumb ass straight for one damned minute!" Then, as if suddenly prompted by an inner demon he could not understand and no longer wanted to control, turned to Tucker and grabbed him by his throat and punched him once again in the mouth, "I've told you for the last time about callin' me that. The next time that word comes outta your stinkin' mouth, be you faded or just bein' too smart for your own good, you say that where I can hear it, and I'll beat your ass 'till you can't walk. Now," Billy calmed himself he returned to the topic foremost in his mind, "how do you know he works in a dress store?"

"Damn it, Bill," Tucker attempted to complain as he spat blood. "Cause... I saw him goin' in... there the other... day... carryin'... stuff," Tucker stammered as he stopped to extract a rotted tooth loosened by his drug of choice and Billy's latest blow. "Damn, Bill, you didn't have to smack me twice. I think... I only said it... once."

"Yeah, well, you said it one too many times, you dumb ass. Now, settle down and listen before you answer me. Why do you think that guy works where you say you saw him go in carryin' stuff?" demanded Billy commanding Tucker's attention.

"Didn't come back out all the time I watched from the courthouse lawn. I watched maybe over two hours, anyway. It looked like he was gettin' chummy with one of them women there, both of 'em laughin' and carryin' on, kinda grab-assin' with each other. I could...see 'em grab-assin' through...the...through the... window," Tucker answered struggling to regain composure.

"Well, we need to find out a little more about that gimp-ass," mused Billy. "I think we may have some business to discuss that he won't find so damned chummy."

"What are you talkin' about Billy? What kind of business do we have that needs discussin' with a dress shop crip?" asked Tucker as his mind became more lucid and he began to forget about his tooth and bleeding mouth, smashed by the person he considered his only friend.

"First things first, Tuck. Let's find out more about that dress shop. Then we'll figure out his name so we can present and discuss our business in a proper manner fittin' the occasion," he concluded in a caring, confident tone as he helped Tucker to his feet.

CHAPTER 16

Daniel planned to ask Ogden about the Purple Heart and Distinguished Service Cross whenever he felt the timing was opportune. "I may ask," he thought, "but he won't likely be willing to go into much detail concerning his military service." He hadn't been back to see Ogden's for almost two weeks due to his friend "being a little under the weather," according to Jane when she called to postpone their meeting. When she called to invite him back to the house, he mistakenly expected Ogden to be in about the same physical condition as he was at the conclusion of their last meeting.

As had become routine, Jane met him at the front door and escorted him into the same comfortable room where Ogden usually sat in a recliner. Daniel was surprised to find Ogden propped up in a half-sitting, half-lying position on the couch. Ogden's physical appearance instantly announced that his friend's condition had deteriorated since they last met. He studied Ogden's eyes and recognized that unmistakable roundness and hollowness indicating the cancer had progressed to a point approaching hopelessness.

"Come on in, Dan," Ogden stated trying to hide the obvious weakness that was rapidly overtaking his body. "As you can see, I've had a few rough days since you were last here," he volunteered as he shifted himself on the couch attempting to find a position that would be more welcoming and allow him to converse with his guest.

"I hope you are feeling better now," Daniel replied casually, trying not to telegraph the shock he was feeling at seeing his friend in an alarmingly weakened condition.

"Daniel, let's not disregard or try to ignore the truth. You know, Jane knows and I, most of all, know this thing isn't going to let loose of me now. Do I feel better? Compared to what? I feel better than I did before Jane gave me my morning doping. I feel strong enough, right now, to continue with our business, at least for a time. But let's get on with it before that 'feeling better' feeling disappears," he stated pointedly.

"You start talking and I'll write," Daniel answered forcing himself to smile as he once again attempted to overcome Ogden's apparent depressed mood.

"When I found the bag, I sensed someone was watching me. I told you that earlier," Ogden began immediately. "After months without hearing anything from any source concerning such a large amount of cash being lost, I came to think my gut feeling had been wrong. One night, along about two o'clock in the morning, the front door bell woke us both from sleep. I walked across the hallway to look outside through a bedroom window and saw a sheriff's patrol car parked in our driveway with the lights flashing. I figured, somehow, I had been found out," he paused to re-shift himself.

"Ogden," Jane said as she entered the room and sat down, "I can tell Dan the rest of what happened with the deputy sheriff that night if you need to rest for awhile."

"That seems like a good idea, sweetheart. I do need to rest for a minute. Maybe I'll gain a little strength in the meantime," he replied as he looked kindly toward his wife then reclined on the fresh pillows Jane had brought with her.

"Ogden opened the front door, ready, he told me afterward, to cooperate fully with the police. However," she paused for a sip of coffee, "the officer had stopped to let us know we had left a dome light on in the car Ogden had left outside for the night. That was it! Just a kind, though from our perspective, a disturbing gesture from a young man trying to be of service. Ogden thanked him, went outside to turn the interior light off and returned to bed. You can bet we were both relieved with how that episode turned out," she smiled; conveying relief their brush with the law had been inconsequential.

"Well," Ogden now continued as he pulled himself upright, "while dodging that bullet turned out to our satisfaction and relief, that wasn't to be the end of the story. Almost two years after I found the money, Jane received an anonymous telephone call at the store. How this character determined I had a connection to Jane's store is still a mystery to me. Anyway," Ogden seemed invigorated, "some guy called and asked to speak with…Jane you can relate this part better than I," Ogden offered.

"As Ogden said, I answered a call one day from some man wanting to speak with 'Mr. Royal.' I remember replying that Mr. Royal didn't work with me but the fellow wouldn't hear any of that. He insisted I give Ogden a message. Again, I explained, attempting not to admit or divulge any connection with Ogden to such a random caller, the person he asked about was not an employee of the store. Then," Jane's tone of voice indicated the fear she had felt and was now reliving, "the caller said I damned well better get a message to Ogden regardless of where in hell he worked because they had important business to discuss and that he would go to the police if Ogden failed to return his call. He left his number, said it was his cell phone, and emphatically told me to have Ogden call him tomorrow…or else.

"He finished by saying he knew where to find me and didn't like fancy rich bitches anyway. He added that he and one of his friends would pay me a visit if he didn't get a return call," Jane finished, her lower lip now quivering as she turned her attention toward her husband as he again shifted himself seeking a different, if only temporary, resting position.

Billy, once again, had leaned on his mother for enough money to buy a pre-paid cell phone as he wasn't in a financial position to subscribe to a monthly service. As usual, fearing a beating or verbal abuse from her unpredictable son, Mrs. Merritt scraped up the few bucks her son demanded. "After all," she thought, "at least he won't be tempted to steal the money he needs and run the risk of being arrested and end up costing me even more money that I cannot afford."

"I called Ogden at his office immediately after talking with this character," Jane continued. "I repeated what I had been told and gave him the number I had been given. Ogden said he would think it over and we would talk it over at home later that evening. Really," Jane considered, "Ogden didn't seem agitated or overly concerned by getting such a message from an unidentified, threatening caller."

"How I sounded and how my guts churned after hearing what Jane told me were not in the same league with each other," he added seemingly brightened by recalling the incident. "I knew the return call had to be made but I decided to wait until the next day. Didn't want to appear overly anxious, you know? After all, there was no way to know, at that time, what we were dealing with. Could have been just another nut out for a few laughs at our expense," he stated as he strained, once again, to pull himself to a different sitting posture.

"The following day, around eleven that morning, I stopped at a pay telephone and dialed the number Jane had given me. I didn't want our home number, or my office number exposed to this guy. He already had found Jane's business number and that, to me, was alarming. After ringing several times, a man answered with a 'Yeah?' I told him I was the person someone at this number had called for yesterday. According to a message I had received, I told the person on the other end, I was responding to a request to return a telephone call. I asked if he was the person that had made the call and if I was speaking with the correct party," Ogden explained.

"If you're Ogden Royal you're speakin' to the right person," the sleepy-sounding man replied.

"Yes, this is Ogden Royal," I answered. "With whom am I speaking and what do you want?"

"It's none of your business who I am. It's what I want that should concern you," Billy, becoming alert, snapped a reply. "You're the gimp I saw loadin' a bag into the trunk of a white car a while back. You were walkin' around the football stadium one evening and I watched you. I know what was in that bag. I didn't put the two things together until a couple of months ago when I saw you walkin' across Kirkwood headed into Nick's. You're the guy, alright. The smartest thing you can do now is to share some of that loot," Billy recited almost as if he had prepared what he would say.

"Unless you tell me your name, I'm hanging up. You can do as you wish. I have your number. I can have the police find you and I will press charges for whatever offense that applies. I don't know what you're getting at, but you have five seconds to tell me your name, beginning now," Ogden instructed the man as he began counting backward from five, followed by four, three, two…

"Billy Merritt's my name, if that's all you want to know and if it's any of your damned business," Billy shot back just before Ogden completed his countdown. The last thing Billy wanted was a grilling from the police for any reason.

"Now, Billy," I countered in a soothing voice, "that wasn't too difficult was it?" Ogden said he had no intention of hanging up without learning more about the caller but he was pleased to learn Billy was seemingly easy to bluff.

"Oh, I want to know, need to know, much more than just your name. After all, I want to treat you fairly concerning whatever it is that is bothering you. What do you want from me, Billy?" Ogden pressed the issue.

"I want some of that money you stole. If you don't shake loose, we'll make you and your cute little wife wish you had," Billy promised.

"Who is the 'we' you just mentioned, Billy? You stated yesterday that you and your friend would pay my wife a visit unless I returned your call. Who is this friend, Billy?" Ogden said he asked in a calm voice.

"I have plenty of friends, don't you doubt that. One 'em is crazy and likely to do anything I tell him to do. Billy stalled not wanting to identify Tucker Warren by name.

"Same drill, Billy. You must learn to be more cooperative if you want to deal with me. You have five seconds to give me the name. Starting now…"

"Alright! Damn! Enough of that bullshit, ass-backwards countin' crap. His name is Tucker Warren," Billy replied hastily.

"Okay, Billy," Ogden continued. Now back to the bag you say you saw me load into a car. You are correct. You did see me place a satchel or a gym bag into the trunk of my car. Now, listen to me carefully. There was nothing of any value in that bag. Just a few rocks and papers some kid taking a geology class had misplaced. Now, Billy, what else do you want from me?"

"I want some of your money, you dumb, lyin' asshole," Billy snarled.

"Billy, I'll say again what I just now told you. There was nothing in that gym bag of any value to me or to you. I found a worn-out, beat-up bag half-full of worthless rocks. How can I give you what I don't have? Ogden asked testing Billy's resolve.

"You people have money. That fancy dress store you own, the way you dress yourself. Yeah, I'd say you are rich. Tell you what, I'm easy to get along with. Give me ten grand, cash, and you'll never hear from me again. Keep messin' me around and I promise you more trouble than you can imagine or handle. What's it to be? You can either shake loose of what I want or let that purty little wife of yours take the punishment," Billy bravely threatened.

"Ten grand? My goodness! Billy, that's a lot of money," Ogden countered while ignoring Billy's emphatic promise to harm Jane. "I cannot possibly come up with what you are asking. I simply do not have that much money to give you or anyone else," Ogden had replied hoping to convey his surprise at an amount of money obviously considered substantial by the would-be blackmailer.

"I don't give a rat's ass where or how you get the money, and I ain't askin' you. I'm tellin' you! Ten grand cash and we're even. Cash. Got it?" Billy quickly responded as if assured he had gained control of the negotiation.

"Let me think for a minute, Billy. Tell you what. I'll call you back tomorrow after I see what I can do about getting some amount of money put together. Give me a day and I'll try to come up with something. Billy, we don't want any trouble from you or from your friend. I'm a man of my word, so I will get back with you tomorrow at about the same time. Is that agreeable with you, Billy?" Ogden assuaged Billy's impatient demeanor as he dropped another coin in the telephone.

"Okay. Yeah, tomorrow, same time and I don't wanna hear about some amount of money. Ten-grand works for me and not a penny less. I'm a man of my word, too, so you keep that in mind. Remember, if you don't call or come up short, my friend will get mighty nervous," Billy reminded Ogden of the threat he had made involving Jane.

"I'll call you, Billy. Now you take it easy and give me a chance to see what I can do. Good bye," Ogden ended their conversation feigning concern for Billy's well-being.

"What did you do after you made contact with Billy?" Daniel asked.

"I sure wasn't planning to give old Billy-boy any money. That was one thing for certain," he replied in a stern voice. "I took my car to a local shop and had a remote device installed that would start the engine, turn on the lights, sound the horn and rev the engine, all from a distance of up to three-hundred feet. Thought those neat features might come in handy as I figured out how I would deal with Billy and Tucker. Dr. Dan, I took Billy's threat toward Jane seriously. I was scared for her safety. I had to play along with this man just to keep him occupied and thinking about all that money he apparently assumed he would soon have. If he remained fixated on getting his hands on our money, he wouldn't be so eager to carry out his threat to harm Jane. At least, that was my hope," Ogden explained.

"Ogden," Jane whispered as she touched her husband's arm, "do you think that's enough for this morning? Are you free tomorrow morning?" she asked turning toward Daniel. "I think it's time for Ogden to take a break."

"Sure," Daniel answered. "Tomorrow, about the same time works for me. Give me a minute while I catch up and I'll move along." He drove back to his home almost trance-like, thinking of what Ogden may have done that satisfied Billy and Tucker.

64

The next morning, Daniel found Ogden sitting in his usual chair appearing to be much stronger than the day before. "Dr. Dan, before we continue…Jane can you come in for a minute?" Ogden called out in a clear and strong voice.

As he was preparing his notebook, Daniel paused to tell Ogden how much better he appeared that morning compared to the day before. "It seems as though you are up and at it this morning," he offered to reassure his friend.

"Dr. Dan, are you trying to pee on my boot then tell me it's raining?" he offered in a light-hearted tone. "I'm up, alright. As far as being at it, as you say, well, that train has already left the station. Minute by minute, day by day has become my time horizon. Some days, thankfully, are better than other days. Lately, none have been anything near good."

Jane entered the room carrying a tray with a pot of coffee and two cups. As she sat the steaming vessel down, she turned to Ogden with a smile, "Is that what you needed, my dear?"

While Ogden seemed in better spirits this morning, Daniel couldn't keep from noticing Ogden's eyes that were not any less rounded or receded this morning. However stronger his old friend was feeling today, he knew a transitory improvement was not to be taken as a reliable indicator of survival. That acknowledgement, once again, brought back a sad memory of how his father had fought so bravely only to succumb to the inevitable.

"Thanks, dear," Ogden, appeared to have rallied, replied in a gentle tone. "I'm sure we'll need some coffee as we proceed but I was wondering if now would be a good time for you go for groceries, pick up my medication at the pharmacy and do whatever shopping you have in mind. Dr. Dan will be here with me and I'm sure I'll be fine. I feel much better today than I did yesterday morning. As Dan just said before you came into the room, 'I'm up and at it!'" he laughed, seeming to enjoy a gentle chiding of his friend.

"Sure. Let me get my grocery list and coupons and I'll be on my way. I should be back at least by lunchtime. Can you two fellows think of anything I can get for you before I leave?" she asked seemingly anxious for even a brief respite to her usual confinement.

"Can't think of anything else we could possibly need or want. Just be careful, and Jane…take your time. I know you need a change from these close quarters I've created for you. If I get tired, I'll let Dan know or I'll just take a nap while he's sitting there," Ogden chuckled.

As Jane pulled out of the driveway, Ogden took a sip of coffee and said, "Dan, it's good for her to get out of the house. She needs a break from time to time just as anyone would. But, really, I wanted to tell you, as they say, 'the rest of the story' that I have never told anyone else."

"You haven't told anyone, including Jane, what you are about to tell me, O.R.? Is that right?" he asked dismayed by what he had just heard and concerned with what he was about to hear.

"You are the first and only person who has heard what I'm going to tell you this morning. As I told you earlier, how you decide to handle this matter will eventually be up to you. In the meantime, what you are about to hear must be held in strict secrecy.

Are we still on the same page with that?" he asked, staring into Daniel's eyes without blinking.

"I hear you, Ogden. I understand what you want and I will follow your instructions…to the letter," he offered feeling uncomfortable by Ogden's fixed, piercing stare.

Ogden then proceeded to tell Daniel about the telephone call he had made to Billy the next day, as he had promised. The first utterance from Billy's mouth was to ask if Ogden had "his" money. Ogden replied that, yes, he had what Billy needed but they must now arrange a place to meet. Ogden asked Billy if he had any suggestions where they could meet that was out of the view and earshot of people that might pass by. Billy suggested various locations that were all too public for Ogden's liking and purpose.

"No, no, no, Billy. We cannot meet in places such as those to conduct our business. Listen, I know a good place for us to meet for a few minutes. Are you familiar with Highway 446 east of town, right off the highway to Nashville? Do you know the bridge that crosses the Lake Monroe causeway at the bottom of the long hill?" Ogden asked.

"Yeah, I know the place you're talkin' about," Billy answered. But there's a problem with that. I don't have a car so how in hell I'm I supposed to get all the way out there?" he snapped, becoming loud and agitated.

"Billy, do you recall what you told me about getting the money you demanded? You told me you didn't give a rat's ass where or how I got the money. Do you remember telling me that, Billy? Well, now I'm telling you the same thing! I don't care how you get there but I will tell you where to be and what time to be there. I'll be there, so if you want what you say you believe you have coming, be there and be on time. Do you understand me, Billy?" Ogden explained he had decided to direct this undertaking to his advantage.

"Billy," Ogden continued, "I'm a crippled old man. I can't walk far or fast or stand for long periods of time. You said you noticed my limp. Well, my disability is worse now than it's ever been. Write down what I'm about to tell you. Here's where and when you and your friend Tucker, both of you and only you two, will meet me," Ogden commanded.

"Wait a minute, you prick. I need to find a paper and a pencil. Give me a second," Billy sputtered becoming pliable to Ogden's controlling demeanor.

"Okay, are you ready, Billy? Go out east of Bloomington on Highway 46. You'll pass the College Mall, of course, and be headed toward Nashville. Turn right onto Highway 446, then you'll be headed toward Lake Monroe. Go across the bridge at the bottom of the long hill. That's about six miles after you make a right turn off Highway 46 onto 446. Do you have that information down, Billy? Okay, after you cross the lake bridge, you will turn left onto the first road that runs along the lake. Drive on back about a quarter mile. You'll see a place where you can pull over on the right side of the graveled road. Be there at nine o'clock sharp tomorrow evening. If you are late, I'll be gone. If you bring anyone with you except Tucker, the deal is off. Do you understand what I've told you, Billy? Do you have any questions?" Ogden wanted to make certain Billy understood his directions.

"I got it. I know the area. I've lived around here all my life. Do you think you're talkin' to an idiot, or somethin'?" Billy sounded offended.

66

"No, no. Just wanted to make sure you will get to the right place at the right time. After all, we don't want to slip up and miss each other. Billy, as I told you, I'm a crippled old man who doesn't want any trouble with you. I'm trying to meet your demands. Let's get this done quickly and we'll both be on our way. Is that fair to you?"

Ogden said he had wanted to seem somewhat agreeable to Billy's demands. Ogden intended to fortify Billy's over-confidence by sounding fearful and by reiterating the marked prey was old and infirm.

"I'll be where you said and when you said, you can bet on it. Only thing I'll say is, you'd better be there with the money or you'll find out I ain't jackin' around with you or your wife," Billy answered as he angrily snapped at the button that ended their conversation.

Ogden went on to tell how pleased he was Billy had assessed him as a weak, defenseless cripple. "It's always to your advantage to be underestimated regardless of the matter at hand," he surmised.

The location described to Billy for the meeting place was familiar to Ogden. He occasionally fished from that area of the lake and he had surveyed the location he specified to his unsuspecting prey earlier that morning. At that time of year, now past Labor Day, only sporadic boating activity took place even during daylight hours. At night, that locale should afford the degree of privacy and seclusion he desired. "Just the two blackmailers and me," Ogden thought, excited by the impeding challenge.

"I arrived almost two hours early," he explained. "I wanted to be there and get a few things in order beforehand. Write my 'op order,' as we used to say in the Army. I hid my car about seventy-five yards, or so, beyond the pull over spot I had described to Billy. Then I selected a relatively comfortable place to sit near the pre-arranged meeting place and hid in the brush. I wanted to be close enough to hear what they might discuss when they arrived and yet far enough away not to reveal my presence," he went on seemingly gaining energy as he recounted the episode.

"I take it you didn't bring money with you?" Daniel asked, seeking to confirm Ogden's vow that he wouldn't give Billy any money.

"Just a few bucks I usually carry in my wallet. No. Those two were going to get what they deserved but surrendering any amount of money to them wasn't factored into my way of thinking. I brought an old briefcase partially filled with newspapers, a K-bar knife and an unregistered 22-caliber pistol with a silencer attached and a pair of latex gloves. Oh, I also carried my 9mm semi-automatic pistol loaded with fifteen rounds and two magazines in reserve, just for good measure. Preparation, Dan, you know all about that necessity. The briefcase was simply a prop, a diversion for those two. Why did I bring the knife and the pistols? Well, I thought I had reason to bring those tools along," Ogden sat back to allow Daniel opportunity to record what he had said.

"Daniel," Ogden suddenly continued in a pensive voice, "how long do you think ten grand would have kept those two off our backs? I don't think Billy and Tucker would have been satisfied until they had bled us dry. Then, who can say what they would have done after that? Billy had made a serious threat that he would harm Jane. I take a man at his word. I wasn't about to allow those two any opportunity to terrify or harm my wife. If Billy had threatened me, that would have been a different matter. But...he promised to seek revenge against the one person I love dearly."

During a pause that allowed Daniel opportunity to bring his notes current, he remarked to himself concerning Ogden's calm demeanor. "Here is a man who is about to tell me something I cannot imagine and yet he seems perfectly at ease with himself and with whatever he did."

"I was relying on two basic military tactics while I waited for Billy and Tucker that evening," Ogden recalled. "I had prepared the area and the equipment I believed I needed for our meeting. If I could divide Billy and Tucker for even a brief time, they would be easier to conquer. If I could introduce the element of surprise, my chance of a clean, successful operation would become more likely. I visualized and mentally rehearsed how I would employ my strategy as I waited silently for the hunters who had unknowingly become the prey."

"Along about ten minutes to nine, an old beat-up Cushman motor scooter sputtered off Highway 446 onto the lane where I was waiting. Onboard were two bedraggled and frail younger men. Once they were certain they were on the correct side road, Billy sitting at the front, killed the engine and both men got off. Dr. Dan, I was shocked by how downtrodden and thin those two were. I almost felt sorry for them, but that emotion quickly passed as I recalled the threats they had made concerning Jane. But, it wasn't until they began talking that they confirmed what I had to do."

Billy, Ogden recalled, began lecturing Tucker to keep his mouth shut during whatever exchange he imagined might take place. "I'll do the talkin' and you do the listenin' and that's all you are to do. Got it, Tuck?" Billy seemed to be nervous and in his customary foul mood.

"I ain't sayin' nothin' 'bout nothin', Billy. Wonder what's keepin' the gimp, though. Hope this ain't a set-up and the cops will wheel up and bust us. Say Bill, where'd you steal this scooter?" Tucker asked incapable of concentrating on the more urgent matter at hand.

"Shut up, Tuck! Who gives a damn where I got this pile of junk scooter? Does that really matter so much to you? If anyone other than Royal pulls in here, that ain't our scooter. Shove the damn thing over there off the road, as if somebody else left it here. If a cop shows up, we'll tell 'im we were hitchin' a ride back to Bloomington and walked off the highway hopin' to find a phone 'cause mine went dead," Billy impatiently explained as he coached Tucker while surveying his surroundings with darting, beady eyes.

"No, not really, Bill. I was just askin' you about it. That's all. Wonder why the gimp ain't here, though," Tucker pouted remaining fixated on his earlier concern.

"Oh, he'll be here," Billy reassured and consoled his partner. "Now, remember our plan. We get the money and the crip gets what's coming to him, the smart ass. Then we'll call his little wife and tell her we've got her lover boy. If she wants him back, we'll need a few more bucks for the favor," Billy was becoming almost giddy as he explained his plan for probably the tenth time to his incapacitated accomplice.

"But... Bill..., if we waste this guy, how can we... why will we need to get him back to his wife?" Tucker asked, still oblivious to the point of Billy's plan.

"Leave it to me, Tuck. The point is, Tuck, he ain't never comin' back to his little missy tonight or ever. We'll get lots more money from his wife and off we go. She'll do as we say. I could tell she was scared of me when I talked to her on the 'phone. If she thinks we have her husband, she'll be happy to pay big bucks to have him returned. She won't know he'll already be worm food by the time we call her. Now sit down, shut up and listen for him to pull in," Billy once again explained his plan to Tucker.

"At that point, I was convinced of what I had to do," Ogden stated flatly. "Those two punks intended to kill me and blackmail Jane for even more money. If I ever doubted how I would handle Billy and Tucker, overhearing their violent plan removed all question in my mind."

"After overhearing Billy and Tucker's plan, I moved closer to where I had hidden my car. When I reached a pre-planned location, I pressed the remote button that started the car's engine. I then pressed another button that sounded a short blast of the car horn."

"What in hell was that and where did it come from?" Tucker asked jumping to his feet.

"How in hell should I know, Tuck? Sounds like somebody started a car and honked the horn. You take this flash light and walk up there a ways and have a look," ordered Billy.

"Dan, sometimes a situation works out better than could ever be imagined! I could barely believe Billy and Tucker had so easily complied with my plan. They were unwittingly dividing themselves. The conquer aspect of that plan was about to unfold," Ogden added as if he was teaching a basic infantry course.

"Tucker murmured something about snakes then hesitantly grabbed the flashlight from Billy's outstretched hand and proceeded to walk slowly in the direction to where my car was parked," Ogden recounted. "As he walked around the curve and out of Billy's sight, I tossed a small pebble that landed on the opposite side of the road of where Tucker was ambling toward my location. The pebble startled Tucker. As a reflex, he jumped to the side of the lane where I was waiting. As he turned to continue walking, I jumped him. With my left hand firmly over his mouth, I whispered for him to keep quiet.

"In a very low whisper, I asked Tucker what he was looking for and he gurgled something about a telephone. Whatever he was trying to say would be the last words he would ever speak. With a quick and forceful snap, I broke his neck and Tucker slumped quietly to the ground. I thought about using the knife but decided to wait a few minutes to make sure the neck snap had been fatal. There wasn't any reason to spill blood, leave evidence, unnecessarily. I waited a few minutes and then felt for a pulse but Tucker had expired. Now, I thought," Ogden seemed to gain energy as he recounted that night near Lake Monroe, "there was Billy to satisfy."

Ogden reclined and collected his thoughts as Daniel recorded how Tucker had met his demise. While writing feverishly, he weighed what his friend had done against his own sense of right and wrong. "How would I have handled this matter? How should I feel about Ogden now that he is a confessed, premeditated killer? What would I do if someone threatened Lucy as Jane had been threatened?" As he grappled with his conscience to answer that question honestly and permanently, Ogden seemed anxious to continue.

"I placed Tucker's filthy, worn baseball cap on my head and picked up the flashlight he had been carrying along with the briefcase I had brought with me," Ogden interrupted the quiet that had fallen as Daniel sorted through what he had just heard. "As I walked around the curve in the road, I saw Billy standing, straining to see who was coming toward him. Blinded by the light I directed into his eyes from Tucker's flashlight, Billy mistook me for his partner. 'Tuck, get that damn light outta my eyes, you asshole,' Billy complained.

"Tuck will be with you in a few minutes," I answered while walking toward Billy.

"Hey, who the hell... are you?" Billy, now surprised by a different voice than he expected, asked in a high-pitched, excited tone.

"I'm Ogden Royal, Billy," I answered him in a non-threatening manner. "Tucker is off in the weeds. Said he needed to relieve himself. Don't worry, you'll be together again in a few minutes," Ogden recounted calmly.

As Ogden drew closer, Billy started to reach behind his back with his right hand. Ogden assumed Billy, caught off guard, was frantically groping for a weapon. "Billy," Ogden evenly directed as he revealed the pistol, "place both hands on top of your head and stand perfectly still. Do not move from where you are standing. Do you see I have brought a briefcase? I have what you want, so just relax. Now, do as I say and we'll get this finished without any problem."

Billy, as ordered, placed both his hands on his head, as his mind likely remained focused on the big payoff he anticipated about to take place. "Okay, Billy," Ogden counseled as Billy stood still with both hands in view, "now get down on your knees. No, no! Don't take your hands off your head. Get down... now!" Ogden directed sternly and Billy once again complied with that forceful yet composed command.

"Billy, are you a man of your word?" Ogden asked.

"Yeah. I do what I say I'll do," Billy answered. "Now give up the money and Tuck and I will get outta here...hey...what's the pistol all about?" Billy stammered as Ogden place the barrel of the weapon between Billy's eyes.

"I take you at your word, Billy. You say you are a man who does as he promises. Too bad you promised to harm my wife, Billy. Too bad you and Tucker had planned to kill me and blackmail my wife. Now, Billy, I'm going to give you exactly what you deserve," he stated without emotion as he pulled the hammer back on the pistol that was resting squarely between Billy's eyes.

"I... didn't mean it...just bull crap," Billy began to blubber. "I'll never bother you or your wife again. I promise. Just let me go. Don't... do this...please. I'm beggin' for my life..." Billy, realizing his great disadvantage, now openly quaked and sobbed.

"I am saddened I cannot, will not, grant your request, Billy. You two messed with the wrong gimp or crip, as you both called me. No, Billy. Your sorry life ends here, tonight. Just like Tucker's life ended a few minutes ago. That's right, Billy. Your friend Tucker is dead. I, a crippled old man, killed him with my bare hands and you didn't hear a sound. How does that make you feel, Billy? Doesn't it make you feel stupid to have been lured into a fatal trap by a person such as you took me to be? With the silencer on the end of this pistol, nobody will hear the shot that brings your miserable life to a just ending," Ogden then repositioned the pistol to the top of Billy's head.

"Billy, I want you to know something. Shut up your cowardly blubbering and listen to me. You guessed right about what you thought was in that bag you saw me load into my car. Billy, there was well over a million dollars in that bag. Think of all that money, Billy. The ten grand you demanded was unimportant to me. We wouldn't even have missed that piddling amount.

Billy, you have said several times you are a man of your word. You've made that claim each time I've spoken with you. You do as you promise. I have to believe you about that. I just wanted you to know you made one correct call in your life when you figured out I had all that money," Ogden said to offer Billy one last positive thought.

"Please...can't...you...just...let...me...go?"   Billy   asked   now   crying unashamedly.

"No, Billy. That's not how this is going to end. This going to end right here, this evening, right now," Ogden whispered as he slowly pulled the trigger and Billy collapsed forward.

Ogden then removed the license plate, carefully wiped the scooter with his handkerchief to eliminate Billy and Tucker's fingerprints and then removed a length of cotton cord wrapped around the seat post, evidently brought along by Billy to restrain the intended victim. Then he pushed the Cushman to the bridge and lifted it over the railing. With a splash, cool water met the warm engine and emitted small ringlets of steam before the scooter quickly sank out of view.

After he removed Billy's wallet, a knife and a cell phone from the pockets of his soiled jeans, he dumped his body in a nearby abandoned cistern. Ogden noticed Billy had cconcealed a box cutter in his back pocket along with a few more strands of nylon rope. As he had promised Billy, Tucker soon joined him in a watery, fetid grave.

As Ogden drove onto Highway 446 and headed west toward Bloomington, a gentle rain began to fall. Before he arrived home, a heavy thunderstorm stalled over Lake Monroe and washed away all evidence from the site where Billy and Tucker met the disabled Ogden Royal.

CHAPTER 18

If the growing mob of feral thugs that roamed the streets of Bloomington who knew Billy Merritt and Tucker Warren missed them, none of them cared enough to inquire concerning their absence. The two troublesome street mopes had simply vanished without notice or alarm.

Billy's mother worried and waited until her son hadn't returned to her apartment for over a week before she contacted the police. Billy often stayed away from home for a few days without word or contact, but after eight days passed without sight or word, her worry became overwhelming.

Billy's habitual unannounced return home always seemed to find him in a half-starved condition, needing a bath, clean clothes and rest. After his needs had been satisfied, Billy would resort to his kinder, groveling personality. When he sensed his mother had been duly convinced of his rejuvenated sense of purpose and sincerity, he would get around to expressing what was on his mind. In his customary cunning manner, he would begin by promising to seek gainful employment. In the meantime, he would happen to mention, he needed a few bucks to get started. "Just a little money to get started, Ma," became Billy's tiresome mantra, "and this time I promise, I'll pay you back."

Some missing person reports generate Herculean attention and action from the police. Some, however, aren't given much attention. The city police department took Mrs. Merritt's report, along with the most recent snapshot of Billy, in a kind and professional manner while promising to do all possible to locate Billy. "All possible" didn't turn out to be very much.

The local police department categorized Mrs. Merritt's request for assistance a low priority matter. They would not waste resources conducting a costly search for a known vagrant and troublemaker, as they had, for good cause, labeled her son.

Mrs. Merritt resided on the Westside of town and therefore an involuntary, circumstantial member of the voiceless population of Bloomington, Indiana. If she had been a wealthy resident living on the Eastside or an elitist member of the Indiana University faculty, her request for assistance would have gained credence and would have generated immediate, tireless action. When a wealthy, powerful family requests help locating a missing child, the reputation of the child is not the deciding factor as to how much assistance is forthcoming. The community had always produced the resources necessary to protect the interests of the gentry. As this was not Mrs. Merritt's plight, the sudden, mysterious disappearance of her son was unimportant to those in power. Such is justice and fairness in this college town divided east and west, the have and the have-nots, by College Avenue.

Billy Merritt no longer existed. There was never an official explanation or conclusion to explain his disappearance. As time dragged painfully on, Mrs. Merritt, now sickly and confined to a small government-subsidized apartment, quit calling the officer who once had been kind and considerate. She sensed the officer had become intolerant of "that old woman whose worthless son had probably run away to hide because he owed somebody money."

Tucker Warren was truly alone in the world. He didn't have any relative who cared enough about him to file a missing person report. Both Tucker's parents were alive when he vanished but both had become mired in their own misery compounded by alcohol and drugs. If either parent ever noticed Tucker's absence, they never bothered themselves to contact the police.

"Are you still with me, Dr. Dan?" Ogden asked. "I tried to warn you before we started with this. What are you thinking? You look startled. I didn't mean to assault your senses or catch you by surprise. Hey, I did what I thought best for Jane. This had nothing to do with the money. I don't regret what I did to Billy and Tucker. They were bound to harm somebody at sometime. They received sure and sudden justice. I didn't go looking for anyone to hurt or kill. Those two searched me out. Thought they had an easy mark. Well, it wasn't so easy for them after all."

"You don't need to explain or justify to me why you acted as you did. I don't know that I would have done the same under those circumstances. As far as I'm concerned, I am convinced you believe you acted in self-defense. After all, you overheard them talking about what they had planned for you and then for Jane," Daniel haltingly stated his agreement while his inability to make eye contact belied his words and his shaky conviction.

"Billy and Tucker chose to live as they did. How many second chances do you suppose those two wasted? They both had opportunity to seek better lives. We all do. How long should anyone be allowed to blame other people for their circumstances?" Ogden asked not pausing for a reply. "Sooner, better than later, we all have to make the choice as to which path we take. If we only take time to look around, we will notice people who serve as good examples to follow in order to lead a decent life. Sure, there are those who are bad examples. We should learn from them, too. Learn what not to do, what to avoid.

"Billy and Tucker, grown men, made their choices. They could have found satisfaction and a worthwhile existence if they had been willing make an honest effort and to pay the price. They found the price too high to bring about the changes they needed to make. Those two wanted everything to come to them the easy way, without effort or sacrifice.

"Intending to try anything isn't good enough. Whenever you hear someone say 'I intend to try,' take heed. Most of the time that's a precursor to an excuse for a half-hearted effort. Do as you say you'll do. If you are doubtful at the outset, don't make the pledge to anyone, most of all, to yourself. Giving up harms the quitter most of all. Quitters bear an awful burden when they finally realize the stench and pollution they leave behind by their weakness, their failures. We all fail because certain goals are beyond our abilities. While those failures often bear a sad outcome unto themselves, they are different matters. I'm talking about just giving up because it was expedient at the moment.

"Look at it this way, Billy and Tucker got exactly what they deserved. Do you remember when Sirhan B. Sirhan shot Robert Kennedy in that hotel kitchen back in 1968? How many people saw that murder take place? What term did the media use to describe Sirhan? The term they applied was 'suspect.' A suspect! Why does our society insist on resorting to such inaccurate terminology? Sirhan was not a suspect. He was the man who killed Robert Kennedy. What happened to Sirhan? Did he receive prompt and certain justice? No, he did not get what he deserved. How many lawyers have reaped millions of dollars defending and arguing the case of that cold-blooded killer?

73

"Keep in mind; many members of law-making bodies at the state and national level are lawyers. Legislators write law and they write the laws not always to the betterment of the public but, all too often, to enrich themselves. What would have happened to Billy and Tucker if they had carried out their plan? Those two mutts would have become 'suspects' and some public defender would have fought long and hard, at the expense of taxpayers, to get them off, scot-free, or the best plea bargain possible. In the meantime, Jane and I would have become irrelevant. We would have become voiceless victims. I was presented with an opportunity to make sure they would not harm either of us and that they would be punished for even thinking of such evil.

"Would you rather risk becoming a suspect or a victim? Suspects get to live and victims, well, they very often become lost in the shuffle. You may now think of me as a murdering vigilante or, as I see it, as person who insists on upholding right and wrong. Sometimes, I admit, I remember Billy and Tucker's pitiful, pleading eyes and the sour stench that reeked from their filthy bodies and clothing as I carried them to their grave. Try as I may to forget, their eyes, their horrified, shocked eyes, will remain in my mind forever. I can't forget Billy and Tucker, but I am not remorseful I killed them."

"Well...Ogden, to say the least, you surprised me. I don't think badly of you for what you did as I believe you were acting in what you believed to be in defense of yourself and Jane. I share your frustration with our criminal justice system and our societal bent on how we handle wrongdoers. For sure, many things don't seem right. As I sit here thinking about all this, I believe I would prefer being a suspect rather than a victim, if that answers your question."

"Well, I think that's enough for today. Jane should be getting back here in a few minutes. I believe we'll need maybe two more meetings to wrap this up. Can you come back...wait...was that the doorbell?" Ogden interrupted himself. "Jane would be coming in the backdoor. Dan, will you go to the front door and see who is there and what they want," Ogden directed.

Before the doorbell rang the third time, Daniel opened the door and stood face to face with an Indiana State Police trooper who was holding a woman's purse in hand.

CHAPTER 19

"Mr. …Royal?" the state trooper asked softly, as his halting words belied an effort to disguise his obvious nervousness.

"No…but this is his home. My name is Daniel Tyler. May I help you, officer?" he asked, while eying the purse the officer was unconsciously switching from one hand to the other.

"No, I'm sorry… you can't Mr. Tyler. I need to speak with Mr. Royal. My name is John Edge, Indiana State Police. Please…" the officer paused as he fought to maintain his professional bearing, and then continued rapidly, "please let Mr. Royal know I need to speak with him for a few minutes." Trooper Edge unnerved by his lack of self-control and inexperience glanced downward to the purse that did not feel comfortable in either of his hands.

"Mr. Royal is here but he isn't well. I don't mean to be rude, but please wait here for just a minute. I'll be right back," and with that, Daniel closed the door and retreated to find Ogden sitting ramrod straight, his facial expression attesting to the tension he was sensing while his eyes searched for explanation.

"O.R.," Daniel, apprehensive by watching the officer shuffle a purse he knew he had seen before, announced, "there is a state trooper at the front door who said he needs to speak with you." Daniel felt certain the purse that was causing the trooper consternation did not promise good news for Ogden.

"Whaa…?" Ogden asked through an open mouth as he processed Daniel's words, while searching his friend's face for the answer that would relieve his sudden unease. "A state trooper? Did he say what he wants with me? Well, go ahead…show him in."

As John Edge walked toward Ogden, he extended his right hand and introduced himself. "Mr. Royal," Edge seemed to be slowly choosing the appropriate words, "I'm sorry to tell you, sir…Jane Royal of this address…your wife…I assume, has been in an accident. Sir, it's my sad duty to inform you Mrs. Royal died in the ambulance on the way to the hospital. Sir, I… brought her purse to you. The first officer who responded to the accident had to open her purse to make identification. No other contents have been disturbed. I am so sorry for your loss. If there's anything…"

"What…are you saying…telling me? What…what happened…to Jane?" Ogden interrupted, as his body became rigid and he seemed unable to move.

"Sir, she was making a legal left turn as she came off Union Valley Road onto Highway 46. She had a green light as all witnesses to the accident have verified. A loaded semi-truck, headed east toward Bloomington ran a red light and struck her car while she was making the turn. The driver of the truck has been taken into police custody to undergo various tests to determine his physical condition or impairment at the time of the collision," Edge concisely recited the official summary of Jane's death.

"Where… is… Jane…now?" Ogden asked as his face reddened and his lips began to twitch while he struggled to suppress his emotions. His unwavering stare with tear-filled eyes, remained fixed on the trooper conveying an unmistakable plea for help.

"Sir, Mrs. Royal is at the hospital. You don't need to do anything immediately. I know this is a terrible shock to you. You'll need time to decide what arrangements you want to make. Is there anything I can do for you while I'm here?" the officer consoled.

"No, no… nothing I can think of… at the moment," Ogden hesitantly whispered a reply to the officer.

"If there should be anything, please call me at the post. Here, please take this," Edge said as he handed Ogden his card, "in case you think of any reason to contact me. By the way, I brought the groceries that were in the trunk of your wife's vehicle. I'll leave them on the front porch, if that's alright. An accident report will be available at the county sheriff's office no later than Noon tomorrow. You will find the car she was driving at Waldo's storage lot, on West Seventeenth. I'm sure the local police and both insurance carriers will need to take a look. Without doubt, sir, the car is a total loss," Edge stated as he stood to leave.

"Thank you, officer. You… have been very kind. I appreciate you came to the house to let me know what happened," Ogden, replied as he bravely fought to overcome the shock and confusion he was experiencing.

Ogden remained motionless and unresponsive when Daniel returned to the room after escorting the officer to the door and tending to the groceries Jane had purchased less than an hour ago. "Ogden," he spoke in a soothing tone as he kneeled down alongside his shattered friend and held his inert hand that hadn't moved from the chair arm since the police officer had entered the room, "is there anyone you want me to call? Should I call Lucy to come over? Can I do anything for you?"

"Hand me Jane's purse. I need to find my medicine," Ogden stated as his posture and downward gaze remained fixed. "And, oh, Dan, call Father Brown at the Catholic Church. Jane was a member there and she would want the appropriate rites. Yes, please call Lucy and let her know. If she wants, she can come over here. Other than calling your wife and Father Brown, I don't know anyone else we should notify. Right now, I don't want to talk but I don't want to be alone. Will you and Lucy stay here tonight?"

"Don't worry yourself about being alone tonight. Don't think about being alone unless you want to be alone. You feel free to tell me what you want or need. I'll be here with you. I'm sure Lucy will be willing to help you with meals and whatever else you may need. We'll both be here when you wake up from your nap."

"Dan, go into the back bedroom, straight down the hall, and bring my walker to me. I don't get around very well by myself and I need the thing to get to the bedroom. Then, if you'll bring a glass of water in, I'll take my mid-day medication and lie down for an hour or so."

As they made their way through the hallway, Daniel steadied Ogden's body by gently holding him by his upper arm and shoulder. He kept silent, as the reality of Ogden's physical state would bring tears of despair if he tried to speak. Ogden had become, just as had another hero in his life, thin, frail and nearly helpless.

CHAPTER 20

Daniel and Lucy remained with Ogden throughout the days and nights following Jane's death. After a private ceremony held at the local church, officiated by Father Brown, the burial was at a cemetery in nearby Ellettsville. Ogden did not want an obituary notice published in the local paper. Outside of Ogden, Daniel, Lucy, Tom Arthur and a few members of Jane's church, the death and burial of Jane Royal passed unnoticed. Ogden, now unable to stand or walk unassisted, attended while confined to a wheelchair.

Ogden's will to fight his disease was seemingly lost the moment he learned of Jane's death. Daniel had taken his old friend to see the oncologist a few days after the funeral. During that brief office visit, the doctor prescribed a higher dosage of the medication Ogden had been taking to dull his more frequent, intensifying pain. Daniel noticed the doctor seemed anxious to conclude his evaluation and didn't offer any advice or remain in the examination room any longer than he deemed absolutely necessary. As he rolled Ogden through the waiting room, the office personnel and nurses didn't make eye contact as they busily searched for tasks that required their immediate attention.

Ogden asked Daniel to call Tom Arthur concerning the accident. Within a few days, Arthur telephoned with information concerning the settlement for the car, which was a total loss, and compensation for Jane's accidental death. Ogden didn't want to haggle about either amount and directed Daniel to tell Arthur to settle the matter as quickly as possible. Arthur advised Daniel to call Jane's life insurance carrier to inform the agent where to deliver the death benefit due from her personal insurance policy. The total benefit, which included a rider for accidental death, was payable to Daniel and Lucy, according to the attorney.

The truck driver involved in the accident was free of alcohol and drugs at the time of the accident. He had simply fallen asleep at the wheel due to weariness brought on by a long trip that had originated in Omaha. According to the investigating officer, there was no evidence of skid marks that would indicate the driver had attempted to avoid the accident. Jane's vehicle was tee-boned at approximately forty-five miles per hour by a heavily loaded eighteen-wheeled rig. After concluding the prescribed drug and alcohol screening, the attending physician released the driver from hospital care. As the groggy, confused driver sat in the hallway awaiting instructions from his trucking company, the state police arrested him for involuntary vehicular manslaughter for disregarding a traffic signal resulting in death. The next morning, a judge set a court date and granted bail. The trucking company hired a local attorney to represent their interests and to arrange posting the bail bond. Twenty-seven hours after he caused an accident that claimed Jane's life, the driver was on his way back to Nebraska.

"Ogden, Tom Arthur said Jane had listed Lucy and me as beneficiaries on her life insurance policy. What's that all about?" Daniel asked at the first opportunity he found Ogden seemingly alert and willing to talk.

"Yes. We both made that change. Why have the proceeds payable to me? If we did that, then the money would eventually be included in the estate and you would have to pay tax when we both pass. This way, the benefit comes directly to you two tax-free. Tom Arthur advised we do that for that reason," he explained.

"Well, once again, I'm caught off guard. I don't know how to feel about this or what to say. I had no idea you had done this. Sure, I understand why you did that way. That's not the point. I guess it just surprised me, as I had no idea the extent of your plans. That's all."

"Dan, all we have will be given to you and Lucy. I'm surprised you hadn't figured that out by now. Get used to the idea. You don't need to say or do anything. Not now and not ever. Don't ever think we did anything out of a feeling of obligation or in an attempt to buy your loyalty. You both have been good to stick around here with me without me making the request. I appreciate what you both have done but I'm not giving you anything in an attempt to pay you. It's strictly our choice, rather, my choice now. You don't have to do another thing for me and nothing will change what I just told you. Do you understand what I'm telling you? If you want, you can go home and resume your normal routine. I'll be okay here. If I need you, I'll call."

"I'll do whatever you want but I don't think you should be here by yourself. What do you think about hiring someone, maybe a nurse to stay with you during the day? That way, I could return in the evenings and be here with you all night. Lucy and I can rotate or we both can stay over. Does that make sense to you?"

"Let me think that over. If you'll get my medicine and help me back to the bed, I need to rest. You can take leave during the time I'm asleep. The way I feel, I'll probably sleep for three or four hours. Maybe you should plan to come back later today. Let me think about the idea of a stranger being around and we'll talk more about what is best after I've rested." With that, Daniel helped him to his bed and drove home to discuss the matter with Lucy.

"He needs someone there with him," Lucy agreed. "He isn't able to get around by himself, let alone fix himself anything to eat on those rare occasions when he does eat a little something. I think we need to talk with him and let him know, in certain terms, that we will help him but he needs someone with him around the clock. Dan, do you think he would be better off in a nursing facility?"

"Probably, but he'll never hear of that. He already told me he wasn't going back to the hospital. Said he wants to be home. Lucy, this won't last much longer. He can't hang on much longer. Ogden has lost his will to put up a front concerning his condition. He sleeps most of the time now and when he's awake, he usually just sits and stares.

"He had me take down the display of his military awards Jane made for him. Told me to get them out of his sight and take them to the basement. When I asked him to recount his military service, he said that was yesterday's news and he didn't want to talk about it ever again. At times, he's not the old Ogden I once knew. When he lost Jane, the cancer gained fertile ground throughout his body and mind. Maybe we can talk with him later this evening. Hopefully, we can make some arrangement that will be acceptable to him," Daniel stated.

When they returned later that afternoon, Ogden was awake and wanted to get out of bed. He wanted to shower, a change of clothes and clean bed linens. Daniel helped with the bathing procedure while Lucy tended to changing his bed and doing the laundry. After a light meal, Ogden seemed refreshed and wanted to sit in his favorite recliner. After he and Lucy sat down, Daniel made his plea concerning a suitable, workable care-giving schedule. After carefully explaining their concern for his well-being, Ogden hesitantly agreed that hiring a qualified nurse to be with him during the daytime made sense. Daniel and Lucy agreed to maintain their nighttime schedules. With that arrangement, he would not be alone, at least for any prolonged time.

After that discussion, Ogden seemed to be more alert and talkative than at any time since Jane's death. He appeared, Daniel and Lucy concurred, to be at ease and wanted to talk. After Lucy excused herself to return home to attend to other duties, Ogden caught Daniel by surprise when he stated, "Dan, I believe you asked about my military service a few days ago. If I remember, I told you that subject was one I didn't care to discuss. Is that right?"

"Yes you did. If you want me to know, I'm a good listener. You should know that by now."

"I don't intend to provide a blow by blow description of what happened. You can read the details, if you want, from other sources. What I'll share with you will be a brief snapshot of what I recall. I have never believed I deserved the honor the Army felt I earned. That belief hasn't changed over the years. I did my job and I was lucky enough to survive. Three of my men who were with me that day weren't as fortunate and that fact still makes me very sad.

"This particular incident happened after I had been back in Vietnam for about three weeks. I was working with the First of the Twentieth Infantry, Americal Division, which was operating between the South China Sea on the east and the mountains to the west. Highway One, the main north-south road in what was South Vietnam, ran on the eastern edge of the area of operation. My job was mostly advisory to the battalion commander. Based on my prior tours and experience, the battalion commander felt I was more useful as a recon leader rather than as a commander of a line company. That was his call to make. I was just happy to be with an American unit and was ready to serve where I could be most effective.

"What turned out to be my last mission was focused on detecting what the NVA were doing along the Song Ve, the River Ve, which meanders near Landing Zone Liz, which was located on a hill that served as the battalion fire base. That morning, my scout patrol of eight other troopers airlifted to a small village abandoned by the so-called friendly Vietnamese. We were making our way across a rice paddy as I stepped up on a dike for a better view. The first shot that came out of a nearby tree line was the one that shattered my lower leg. The following barrage killed three of my men instantly. The radio operator lay dead a few feet from where I had fallen. I knew I had to get to the radio to call for support. As I crawled toward the radioman, I heard excited Vietnamese voices coming toward our position. At that instant, I gave hand signals to the other five men to get ready. I was bleeding badly from my wound but knew we were in a fight for our lives. You know, adrenaline works wonders when you're hurt and scared.

"Just as I was able to get myself pulled as close to the paddy dike as possible, one of the enemy soldiers stepped over my position and noticed the other men scattered about. Luckily, he didn't see me and he was taken out as he readied his AK-47 to fire. He never knew what hit him. Oncoming frantic Vietnamese voices continued to come from several directions indicating they were not about to leave without killing, to the last man, my small patrol. When I peered over the dike, I couldn't believe what I saw. I thought at the time we must have wandered into at least a company of NVA regulars making their way south. We had intersected a major re-supply route, as I learned later, as we were making our way across the paddies.

"After effective rifle fire had been placed on the oncoming enemy, I was able to get to the radio and make contact with the firebase. I first called for one marking round and immediately requested fire for effect. The five men who had survived the initial ambush had brought plenty of ammunition and we each carried a LAW. You likely had some experience with those light anti-tank, easily portable weapons, didn't you? By that stroke of luck, we were able to hold our position until the sky was busy with those glorious helicopter gunships and a company of infantry for reinforcement. Before the battle was finished, eighty-four NVA soldiers lay dead. We lost my three men plus four others from the reinforcing company and a door gunner from one of the choppers.

"As it turned out, we had walked into a battalion-sized force. That's no way to gather intelligence, Dr. Dan, I can tell you that."

"He was taken out," was Ogden's unassuming way of avoiding taking what he considered undue credit for saving the life of his comrades as an enemy soldier had readied his weapon to kill them, thought Daniel. Without doubt, Ogden had done far more than kill one enemy soldier that day.

"Thanks for telling me about how you were wounded and a little about why you were awarded the Distinguished Service Cross. From there, you were on your way home?"

"From Chu Lai, I was sent to Japan for surgery. From Japan, I convalesced at Walter Reed. Jane remained close by my side each day during my recovery. I received my discharge papers from the Army after a long rehabilitation period. With this bum leg, I was unable to perform my military duties. I was out on my ear without a marketable skill, at least so I thought at the time."

"One thing for sure, we were prepared to meet whatever the NVA had to bring. We were looking for trouble but we didn't waste time and effort in running our mouths making threats. Anyone who has survived service in a war zone soon learns to anticipate the unexpected. If we hadn't been properly trained, equipped and alert, the end result would have likely been far different. I had good men with me that day and for that, I'm grateful. Each man of that patrol deserved recognition for bravery, not just me.

"Billy and Tucker," Ogden paused as he struggled to change his sitting position, "were dumb, unprepared and undisciplined. They allowed their mouths and their greed to overload their abilities."

Daniel was surprised at Ogden's unannounced, spontaneous shift to a matter he assumed long closed. As he sat making notes, he waited silently to see where this resurrected topic would lead.

"Justice, quick and sure. The intended victim became the judge, jury and executioner. Those were my unwilling roles. If Billy had threatened me and not Jane, I believe I would have reacted, and acted, differently. It seems to me that when a person has conjured and harbors a harmful act to the extreme point of verbalizing a threat against an innocent party, there is no time or reason for debate. Failure to take a man at his word is to invite disaster. I will attempt to reason with a sensible man, to a point, but I will not argue. I wasn't willing to bet Jane wouldn't eventually come to harm at the hands of those two.

"Dan, you know I'm not an expressive person. I don't have a lot to say just to make conversation. I'm sure some folks think I just an uncaring, remote person. For those who know me, I don't think that's the case. It's just not in my nature to bring undue attention to myself.

"As a kid in high school, when I won a wrestling match, I never gloated. I never paraded around the mat lording my skill and determination over a defeated opponent. I displayed the same attitude concerning my military service. I never sought recognition or glory. I have never participated in a Fourth of July parade. I never joined any of the service organizations and never sat for a newspaper interview regaling and explaining why I was worthy of high military honor. I did what I had to do and at times, it was fight or flight. Why should I hold myself out as someone special compared to the young, brave soldiers who weren't even given a proper welcome home? Far too many young men who served in Vietnam were unnoticed, never recognized for their heroism.

"How many stories did you hear about returning soldiers being harassed and spit upon as they walked through airport terminals on their way home from Vietnam? You talk about a perverted sense of gratitude from sorry-assed people. Those young soldiers deserved better treatment than what this country has given them, that's for sure. No...I didn't seek approval or any of the advantages I may have been granted based on service to my country.

"I have never considered myself as a cold or an aloof person. I grew up in a loving home. I've never met any better people than my parents. I loved them dearly and, to this day, think of them often. I was totally dedicated to Jane and her well-being. I don't understand how anyone could love another person more than I loved her.

"I've never asked much of anything from anybody. I respect other people for what they are, fellow human beings. I accept people, faults and all, because none of us can claim perfection. Sure, I found some people more likable than others but I respected everyone.

"I considered it my duty, an obligation, to show decency and respect for people I met in this life. I expected, and I suppose in a very primal, instinctual way, demanded that same respect for myself. We will always meet people we don't understand and, for whatever reason, may even dislike. That's alright as long as we remember that's not an excuse for rudeness or abuse.

"It wasn't the money that cost Billy and Tucker their lives. Billy and Tucker made the fatal mistake of not acting respectfully toward another human being. They saw me as an old, crippled man they assumed they could easily coerce, blackmail and then murder. Sometimes those people who appear to be meek, mild and weak are acting deceptively to their true nature and abilities.

"It seems to me our culture doesn't place much stock in its elderly citizens. People of all age groups, it seems, focus on what they see today in the people they meet rather than considering what the object of their disapproval or disregard may have accomplished in an earlier life.

"I'm sure you have noticed an older crippled man trying to help his elderly wife in a grocery store. At first glance, all you see is an old couple that can't seem to keep out of your way. They're slow to move and they may take a little longer to decide what they want than what a judgmental onlooker may deem acceptable. Were they always as they are on the day you took notice of them? No, they were not. Each one of them was once younger, stronger and may have been highly successful in some area of endeavor. We can learn valuable lessons from older people, but first we must be willing to look beyond their present circumstance and condition.

"If the casual observer, the self-appointed critic, would pause and imagine what life may have brought those old, proud people, they might be surprised at what those two had accomplished as younger people. Perhaps the feeble old woman once served as a nurse during one war or another, helped wounded, homesick youngsters regain some semblance of health. That slow-moving, tottering old man may have been at Anzio, at D-Day, Iwo Jima, Pork Chop Hill or at Khe Sahn, wounded in service to his country and may have earned a high military award for gallantry. That's what our young people need to be reminded of so they aren't so quick to dismiss the old people they encounter.

"Or maybe neither one of them served a day outside the county of their residence. Maybe the old man worked his entire life at a job he hated but never missed a day of work because he was determined to provide for his family. Maybe that old woman never worked outside the home, but she worked very long and hard taking care of children and her husband. Regardless of where or how they served, they are worthy of respect.

"If you don't remember anything else, Dan, keep in mind nobody is ever exactly as they seem or how you imagine or want them to be. Not me, not you, not anyone you will ever meet. I'm sure you remember what we used to say in the Army about making assumptions? Be wary when you catch yourself assuming very much, positive or negative, when you are tempted to judge yourself or other people. Humanity falls far short of perfection and if we expect otherwise, we invite frustration and a guilt-ridden existence.

"I worry about the future of this country. Are we becoming an uncivil society? What do we now hold dear and respect? Certainly not the church as once was the case. Government leaders and elected officials are often ineffective because they have become willing toadies of the electorate just to insure their re-election. Our public school system is weaker because of the unions and because a liberal, permissive agenda has almost won the day. Older people, after working long years and earning a decent retirement, are being demeaned and labeled as liabilities and drains on the economy because of social security and health care issues.

"It seems the common threads that have held us together as a nation are under attack. Whom should we consider unworthy of respect or even basic civility? I'm afraid there will be a high price to pay someday for our inattention to our youthful citizens. Parents have become too busy with their own affairs to pay much attention to the proper instruction of their children.

"I'm not sitting here telling you erosion of respect for certain people and institutions hasn't been deserved. We've had countless episodes of misbehavior from church leaders, politicians, school officials and even the elderly are too often selfish and greedy. We shouldn't hold every individual in high regard. That's not my point. I do believe, however, we are mistreating children when we fail to teach them the values and ideals that have helped make this a great nation.

"If our young people don't feel allegiance or respect for much of anything this country stands for, why should we expect them to defend it? Would you put yourself in harm's way for something that didn't matter to you? In my opinion, we have become so inclusive that we have become fearful to speak against anything. 'If everybody's right, then nobody's wrong,' was a popular slogan during the 1960's. Look around, Dan. There's way too much wrongdoing going on to give credence to that idea.

"As President Truman said, as I recall, 'You might not respect me but you damn well will respect this office.' I think that difference is what we have been missing. We need to become discerning when it comes to punishing wrongdoers without destroying the entire system.

"Billy and Tucker were prime examples of two younger men who failed to learn these lessons because nobody cared enough about them to teach them anything. If they hadn't relied so much on my outward appearance, they might have earned themselves another chance to make something of themselves. If they hadn't been so disrespectful, who knows what they could have accomplished?

"Dan, I believe in ultimate justice. I believe in God though I don't consider myself a particularly religious person to the extent I have ever become a member of a church. I believe I will be held accountable for whatever I've done. Look at me now. It seems as if I am reaping some of what I sowed. Here I am sick, almost helpless and, if not for you and Lucy, a lonely man. Look at what happened to Jane. When I lost her, I lost what I killed two stupid men to protect. When that truck driver fell asleep at the wheel, he inflicted a heavy layer of awful justice. I keep reminding myself I did the right thing with Billy and Tucker. At the time, when I overheard them discuss their plan, I didn't consider other options. I've lived an honest life and tried to do what I considered right. I've also done some things that now weigh heavily on my conscious.

"I believe God makes everything how He wants it to be. I believe the same truth applies to all humanity. We pervert His design with our free will, but He gave that free will to us, too. How I have tried to understand this dichotomy of conflicting purposes over the years. I know I haven't always acted as God intended but I understand perfection is beyond my ability. As I said, my belief in God, in ultimate justice, is unshakeable. When I put Billy and Tucker to death, I knew what I was doing. I was perfectly sane and wasn't acting out of anything near a blind rage. As they would say in court, it was murder in 'cold blood.' I still believe I did the right thing at the time. For their sake, I'm sorry they had to come to such a violent end. I'm not sorry I acted as I did that night. I'm not sorry I prevented them from doing harm to Jane, to me or to whomever would eventually cross their paths. The world is better place without the likes of Billy Merritt and Tucker Warren.

"Do you recall when I told you we wanted some of our good fortune used to help those who need and deserve help?" he quickly changed the subject as if he had created a mental list of items he wanted to discuss.

"Yes, I remember when you mentioned that. I underlined your words that day to serve as a reminder for me to ask you for clarification."

"Do you remember reading in the local paper about substantial cash donations that would mysteriously show up in the Salvation Army buckets at Christmastime?"

"Sure. I don't think they could ever determine the source of that bounty, but, yes, I do remember."

"The source, at least for the sizable and frequent cash contributions, was Jane and I. Believe me, the Salvation Army didn't tell the newspaper reporter about all the money they received from that unknown source. I suppose they didn't want the general public to know just how much we gave them for fear other contributors would decrease their giving. Over the years, we probably donated well over a quarter million dollars, in cash, to that organization. We believe in the mission of the Salvation Army but we insisted on remaining anonymous. They still don't know where the cash came from, or, hopefully, will come from. I hope you will continue with our scheme to help them while remaining unknown and without public notice.

"We gave to Jane's church, of course, and to other legitimate, well-run organizations throughout the community. We did not support political parties or political candidates. We did not support organizations that promoted questionable issues of the day such as abortion for birth control purposes or the celebration of homosexuality. We wanted to support what we believed to be family values and those organizations just didn't seem to square with our convictions. Whatever amount we gave, we always gave in cash, always anonymously and without paperwork to back-up a filing for income tax credit purposes. You see, we have tried to be good stewards of the money. If you agree, I want you to continue, to some extent, in the same vein.

"I would like Mrs. Merritt, Billy's mother, who I believe, still lives on the West side of Bloomington, to be remembered after my death. I don't know how best to handle the matter of giving money to an individual while remaining unknown. Tom Arthur may be able and willing to help you with that. Tom does not need to know why you want to help her or why you want to remain anonymous. If possible, Dan, she deserves some amount of money that will assist her in enjoying some aspect of her advancing years.

"As for the Warren family, I don't know. Same for them if they can be located and workable arrangements made. While I want to help these people, tread lightly and with caution. They, or nobody else, must ever know or suspect the source or the intent of the gift. You do not want to become known by those people for any reason."

"I'll do my best to carry out your wishes, Ogden."

"I've rambled on too long and I'm exhausted. If you'll help me back to the bedroom, I think I need to rest before Jane returns. Bring me one of those capsules and I'll lie down for an hour or two."

"Yes, Lucy will be back here in a few minutes. Do you want to talk more about Jane before you rest? I know this has been a long conversation for you and I know you are very tired. Are you feeling alright, O.R.?"

"I'm... just very tired now. That was just a slip of the tongue by an old man who was remembering his beautiful, wonderful wife. Jane is still very near to me and sometimes I speak her name and I forget she is no longer here with me. Help me to bed and I'll rest until... Lucy... returns."

That exchange was the last lucid conversation Ogden Royal would have with Daniel Tyler or anyone else.

CHAPTER 21

A few days after their instructive conversation, the nurse informed Daniel she believed Ogden required hospitalization. He wasn't eating and slept almost all the time only to awaken for brief moments to call out for Jane. When she attempted to provide medical care, he often became disoriented and nearly hostile. The nurse explained, based on her experience with terminal patients, Ogden's ability to reason was being clouded by the spreading cancer or by the strong medication. Based on his current condition, she strongly recommended immediate transfer to a hospital or to a skilled nursing facility. After Daniel told her Ogden had given specific written instructions, properly witnessed and notarized, that he wanted to live his last days at home, the nurse hurriedly collected her belongings and said she would not return the following day.

"Dan," Lucy whispered as she seated herself next to her husband, "Ogden has me confused with Jane. Whenever I'm in his room, during those brief times he's awake, he talks to me as if I'm Jane. Just a few minutes ago, he told me to call you and ask if you would meet him at Smitty's. I've quit trying to tell him I'm not Jane. It doesn't seem to make any difference. Do you think you should call his doctor and ask if there is anything else we should be doing for him?"

"I called the doctor yesterday morning for that exact reason. Sorry I forgot to tell you. The doctor called back later in the afternoon to ask if Ogden's pain seemed to be getting worse. I told him his pain seems to be controlled but he sleeps most of the time and his mind seems to be wandering. He told me that was to be expected. The nurse had it right. It's either the medication or the disease has spread to his brain. The doctor said, under the circumstances, he is as well off at home as in the hospital. As long as he remains reasonably comfortable, there isn't much more that can be done. I'm sure Ogden left a copy of his wishes concerning his final days with the doctor. Lucy, he can't hang on much longer. This is the hard part. We are simply waiting for the inevitable. If Ogden is lucky, if we are lucky, he'll pass in his sleep and won't suffer. You remember how the end came for my father. He died peacefully and mercifully in his sleep, without word or struggle."

The next morning Ogden again called for Jane. Lucy promptly left the kitchen to see what he needed. "Jane, I think I want some ice cream. That sounds good to me. Do we have any plain vanilla?"

Lucy returned to the kitchen elated Ogden had asked for something to eat. As she quickly sorted through the freezer, she realized she had forgotten to buy ice cream the last time she had gone for groceries.

"Ogden," she said as she walked back into the bedroom, "I need to make a quick trip to the store to get ice cream. Can I do anything for you before I leave? I should be back in just a few minutes. Daniel is on his way and he may be back here before I return. I called him on his cell phone so he knows where I'm headed. Will you be alright for a few minutes?"

"Take your time, dearest Jane. I'll be fine. I don't need a thing except you might bring me a capsule and a little water. You take your time. I know you must need an occasional break from me. Just be careful and I'll rest right here until you get back."

Lucy returned to the kitchen for a glass of water and the plastic bottle containing Ogden's medication. She placed one capsule on his tongue and helped him to a sitting position as he sipped from the water glass. She sat the pill bottle on the nightstand near his bed as she covered his feet with a light blanket. "There now, you rest for a few minutes and think about how good that ice cream is going to taste."

Daniel came back to the house before Lucy returned from the grocery store. Upon entering the house, he assumed Ogden was sleeping so he sat down in the family room and clicked on the television for a quick update on the news. After a few minutes, he heard Lucy's car pull onto the driveway.

"I think he's sleeping. I haven't looked in on him or heard him stir since I came in," he volunteered as Lucy sat the ice cream on the kitchen counter. Maybe we should let him rest and not disturb him. What do you think?" Lucy walked back to the kitchen and placed the frozen container in the freezer then returned to where her husband reclined with the remote control close by his side.

After some time had passed, Lucy went in to check on Ogden and see if he was awake and if he might be ready for a serving of ice cream. When she opened the door and started to step into the room, she stopped in mid-step and shouted, "Daniel, come...here...now! Oh my God, Daniel, I think he's..." Lucy stammered unable to speak the words she knew were true.

"What is it? What's the matter?" Daniel asked as he rushed toward the bedroom then stopped at Lucy's side. There, as if in peaceful sleep in an instinctual fetal position, lay Ogden Royal with his worldly problems brought to conclusion. In his right hand was a gray Ruger semi-automatic pistol, model number P89DC. Lying on the bed where it had dropped from his left hand was a small New Testament. On the side table, the bottle that once held the powerful medication that had helped alleviate his pain was overturned and empty.

"Ogden! Ogden!" Daniel called as he inched closer to the bed. As he stood staring silently at his old friend, he remembered how bravely Ogden had fought and not once had uttered a word of self-pity, complaint or asked why this had happened to him.

Not seeing or smelling blood, he checked for a pulse and listened for breathing. After his quick survey confirmed the obvious, he stepped back from the bedside and stood by his wife's side.

"He's gone, Lucy. I don't know how or what went on here, but he's gone. I'll notify Tom Arthur first then probably, upon his agreement, call the coroner's office. We'll likely need a pronouncement of death and probably an investigation due to the fact a gun is present. I don't know about such matters but we'll do as Tom suggests."

While remaining fixated on the pistol, Daniel stepped to the other side of the bed. He leaned over without touching anything and sniffed the barrel to satisfy his mind nobody had fired the weapon that morning or anytime recently.

"He didn't shoot himself, Lucy. That pistol hasn't been fired in a long time. I'm not going to touch or move anything until the coroner gets here or do whatever Tom advises. I have Tom's number here in my wallet. He needs to know about this before we do anything else. I'm sure he'll provide direction on the best way to proceed." With that, he pulled the sheet up to cover Ogden's body without moving or touching the pistol or the Bible.

Tom Arthur agreed that calling the coroner was the proper course of action. Arthur further advised not to call for the services of any funeral home until he arrived at the house. "He gave me specific written instructions on how he wants this matter handled. I'll bring his directive along with me.

"Dan, I'm so sorry to hear of his death. Ogden was a blessing to all who knew him. He was one of my heroes and exemplified values I strive to emulate personally and in my law practice. I'm relieved to hear he didn't suffer and pleased he had you and your wife close by after he lost Jane. Call the coroner and I'll head that way. I should be over there within a couple of hours."

Ms. Rebecca Ruhl, a deputy coroner, arrived at the house within the hour after Lucy called. Ms. Ruhl quickly determined the pistol, though fully loaded, was immaterial to the cause of death.

"He may have been thinking about using it, but that's as far as that idea went. I'm not going to speculate on his intentions," stated the deputy. "As there are no external wounds on his body, the cause of death was evidently due to complications of advanced cancer. He simply, by my reckoning, overdosed himself. When people are that far along and suffering, their mind sometimes plays tricks on them. He probably woke up feeling uncomfortable and took too many capsules. I found thirty-eight capsules scattered on the floor and the prescription label states there was ninety doses, three per day, filled fifteen days ago, plus what he took this morning and at mid-day. That accounts for forty-seven capsules. So, let's see, forty-seven plus thirty-eight...he must have taken five extra capsules after Mrs. Tyler left for the store. A healthy person could not survive more than three capsules of that powerful drug in one dose.

"My report will read the cause of death as an accidental overdose. In my opinion, there is no need for an autopsy and the record will so indicate. Mr. Tyler, as the deceased's representative, do you want an autopsy performed?"

"No. I agree with you on the cause of his death, but Mr. Royals' attorney, Mr. Thomas Arthur, is on his way over here. If he advises otherwise, what should we do?"

"One of you will need to call the coroner's office before the deceased is transported from the premises. Upon your request for an autopsy, I'll make the necessary arrangements with the hospital. Do you or Mrs. Tyler have any other questions you need answered at this time?"

Daniel and Lucy replied in unison with a barely audible, "No."

"Then I'll be on my way. I'm sorry for your loss. Outside the possibility of an autopsy, my report should be available within twenty-four hours. Take my card and call me if anything should come up that I can help you with."

Turning to address Daniel, Ms. Ruhl advised, "You should take the pistol and unload it before the people from the funeral home arrive. Here," handing the medicine bottle to Daniel as she made her way toward the front door, "you take care of this and his Bible. Be careful with what you do with this medication. This stuff is dangerous and you should be careful that it doesn't fall into the wrong hands. You may want to take it to the pharmacy and they will see that it's properly destroyed. If you want, I can take it back with me and we'll handle it for you. You may want to keep the Bible as a remembrance of him."

"Thanks. No, I don't want to put you to any more trouble. I'll see that his medication is properly disposed of. I'll take it with me the next time I make a trip to the pharmacy."

When Daniel opened the pocket-sized, black New Testament, he saw where Ogden had signed his full name in the space provided on the front inside cover. He recalled many soldiers carried a New Testament throughout their tour of duty in Vietnam. Ogden Royal had obviously treasured his copy and had kept it close inside his bedside table drawer. By signing his name in the space provided, Ogden had, many years ago, declared acceptance and belief in a faith that was evidently meaningful to him throughout his life.

While Daniel had anticipated Ogden's impending death, he was unprepared for the manner in which he died. He was troubled that a bottle containing such strong medication had been left within reach of a disoriented, dying man.

CHAPTER 22

Tom Arthur arrived at Ogden's home a few minutes after the coroner departed. After being introduced to Lucy, he opened his briefcase, retrieved a document and stated, "First things first. I reviewed Ogden's instructions as to how he wanted his burial handled. As you can see here," he indicated pointing to a particular paragraph, "he specifies we employ the services of a small funeral home located over in Worthington."

Worthington, Indiana, a town in Greene County of approximately one-thousand residents, had gained some notoriety when the funeral home Ogden specified began business by advertising their services for as much as seventy percent less than traditional funeral homes in the area.

"Seems they offer a scaled-down, simple, comparatively inexpensive burial service and that's what caught Ogden's eye. You know how he looked out for the dollars. I think we need to give them a call and get them headed in this direction. Are we all in agreement with that?" Arthur asked.

"Let me get a telephone book and I'll make the call," Lucy offered her willingness to help after Daniel nodded agreement while avoiding eye contact with his wife.

"Once Ogden has been laid to rest, I'll need to go over Ogden's will with both of you. In the meantime, while we wait for the hearse, let's have a cup of coffee. Anything else we need to talk about right now, Dan?"

"Lucy, hold up just a second before you make that call," Daniel said arising from where he was sitting. "The coroner asked if we wanted an autopsy performed. My first reaction was no, that wouldn't be necessary. I told Ms. Ruhl, the coroner, I would consult you. She said she is prepared to close her investigation without an autopsy but wanted to give us that option. If there's to be an autopsy, we need to notify the coroner's office before calling the funeral home."

"No, go ahead with your telephone call to the funeral home, Lucy," Tom Arthur directed. "I agree with you. Why go to all that hassle and delay if the coroner is satisfied she has determined the cause, or a contributory cause, of death. I don't see the need to inflict an anatomical dissection on Ogden just to confirm what we already know. We all knew he was dying. As I said, I'm sorry to lose him but, at the same time, I'm relieved his suffering is over," the lawyer offered in a consoling manner.

After two attendants from the funeral home left the house with Ogden's body, Tom Arthur sat down at the kitchen table as he removed a file from his briefcase. "If it's agreeable with you folks, I'd like to briefly go over the highlights of Ogden's will. If this is not a good time for you, we can meet at my office in a few days. This should take just a few minutes. I realize this has been a trying day for you both but now would be a good time to talk and perhaps get an idea of what we are dealing with."

"Sure, now is fine with me," Daniel replied without consulting his wife.

"Whatever you think is best, Mr. Arthur," Lucy offered agreement, sensing her husband's manner toward her had become palpably aloof.

"Well," the lawyer began, "In a nutshell, Ogden's estate will make you two folks wealthy. You may have been wealthy before, for all I know, but you will soon become much wealthier. In short, all their property, their money, their brokerage accounts and the proceeds from Ogden's life insurance policies, which will be a considerable sum, will soon become your assets. I'll notify the insurance carriers to get the claims process started. After I submit the death certificate from the coroner's office, we can expect payment a few days hence.

"As for the property and money transfers, those will entail a little more work and time. If you want, as attorney for the estate, I'll walk Ogden's will through the necessary legal steps for you. I realize I'm not your attorney at this stage. If you prefer, you have the right to hire another lawyer to assist you with this matter. Due to the size of the estate, and the legal details involved, I do strongly suggest you retain an attorney. I'm available to help you if that is your preference."

"Tom, as far as I'm concerned, I prefer you to guide us through this. You wrote Ogden's will and you are familiar with the assets of his estate. You were his good friend for many years. I know Ogden trusted you, and that settles the issue for me."

"I agree. Daniel has spoken highly of you and I think you should handle this matter for us," Lucy added quietly, now convinced she was the cause of her husband's mood swing that culminated in an unspoken hostility directed toward her.

"Thank you. I'm pleased to help you. Now, there will substantial state and federal estate taxes due. Those bills won't come due immediately, thankfully, but they will come due. I'll consult a tax attorney on how we should proceed after I figure out how much we are actually dealing with. Ogden had you both listed as his beneficiaries on his life insurance policies a few days after Jane's death. Life insurance proceeds, unlike the real property and money, will pass to you tax-free. All these matters, except getting the insurance claim process started, can wait until after Ogden's burial."

"Do you have any idea how much money we'll have to pay for estate taxes and legal fees? When will those bills be due?"

"Dan, I'd estimate, as a very rough estimate, almost all of Ogden and Jane's life insurance proceeds will be needed to pay estate taxes and legal fees. Keep that in mind in case you have temptation to make a substantial purchase before we get the estate settled. That's just a guess, but I'd rather you have too much money than be short at settlement time. We certainly want to avoid all the grief the Internal Revenue people can bring to bear on a forced estate sale.

"Ogden and Jane thought of the estate tax problem when they made you and Lucy their beneficiaries. They were hoping you two would have enough money from those sources that you wouldn't be hurried into selling off assets in a fire-sale fashion. Selling when and what you want to sell compared to having to sell something to raise cash…well, I'm sure you can appreciate the difference.

"As I said earlier, this process will require some work and some time. Until the estate is settled, you are off the hook as far as payment of taxes or anything else, for that matter, is concerned. Remember, as we go down this path, there will be substantial taxes and legal bills coming due.

"In the meantime, after a judge has given the go-ahead, we'll have the real and personal property appraised. Then we will sit down and see where we are at and how best to proceed. As I mentioned, you may want to sell some of the real estate property. Did Ogden mention they owned property in Minnesota?"

"Yes, but he never said much about the place except it is located on a lake, off some trail way up north, close to the Canadian border," Daniel replied in a barely audible voice.

"I don't know what the place is worth today, but I do know how much they paid, in cash, when they bought it. What does the princely sum of $341,000, as a purchase price back in 1998 indicate about a possible value today? Probably some amount far in excess of that, I would judge.

"We'll get some advice on how to handle the cash account in Antigua," Tom continued, "You may want to consider simply transferring that account into your names and leaving it there. We'll just have to see what will be most advantageous to you. And, of course, what you are both comfortable in doing. You may not want to deal with those folks down there. I know Ogden and Jane kept that account on a short leash although they did earn a very nice return by taking the risk. We can cross that bridge later.

"Now, have I given you folks enough information to worry you tonight?" Tom Arthur said with a broad smile as he placed Ogden's file back into his briefcase.

"So, Mr. Arthur, you are now serving as our attorney in this matter, from start to finish?" Lucy asked rising from her chair.

"Lucy, please call me Tom. You don't need to observe formality with me. After all, I'm working for you, not the other way around," the lawyer added in a relaxed, friendly manner.

"Yes, I'll be assisting Dan as he serves as executor of the will. And, yes, I'm your representative with this matter. Any questions that may arise, call my office. I'll do my best to keep you both informed as we proceed. As I said, this will take time to work through the system. With Ogden's clear and specific will, a debt-free estate and no living relatives, there's nothing that should be contested. It is my job, my obligation to you both, to make sure everything is proper and legal. You have my promise your best interests will be protected.

"Grace and Paul, my daughter and son that you haven't met, Lucy, will accompany me at Ogden's graveside service," Tom Arthur stated as he made his way toward the front door. "We can all come back here and talk more after the burial, if that suits you. Perhaps we can relax and chat about less serious matters and recall a few favorite stories about our old friend. In a less stressful setting, maybe we can all get to know each other a little better. I'll have Grace bring along one of her delicious chocolate cakes that I think you will both enjoy, that is if you like chocolate!

"One other matter I almost forgot to mention to you. Ogden specified that he did not want his obituary published in any newspaper. Again, old Ogden was ever leery of spending money on anything he considered unnecessary. Keep me posted as to the final arrangements you make with the funeral home. If I'm away from the office, leave the information with Grace or Paul. If you don't have other concerns or questions, I'll be on my way." Tom Arthur stated as he offered his hand to Lucy then to Daniel.

Three days after Ogden Royal died, Daniel, Lucy, Thomas Arthur, accompanied by his two children, and two men from the funeral home comprised the mourners at the graveside service. Those five people, who had known and respected Ogden Royal, with assistance from one of the men from the funeral home, carried his plain pine casket from the hearse to the burial site. The casket sat poised next to a still fresh and grassless final resting place where Ogden had sat silently in a wheelchair and witnessed the burial of his wife a few weeks earlier. According to Ogden's wishes, they had not invited any member of the clergy or representatives from the veteran's organizations. He had made it clear that he did not want the traditional twenty-one gun salute or the American flag draped over his coffin that was traditional for honorably discharged veterans.

As the mourners stood side by side, they fixed their attention on Ogden's stark casket waiting for placement where he would lie next to the woman he had loved. Thomas Arthur cleared his throat that broke a heavy silence and said, "It was my great fortune to have known Ogden Royal since we were both boys growing up on the West side of Bloomington. We attended the same schools. We attended the same church and Sunday school down on South Rogers Street for many years. I think it would be fitting if we bowed our heads and recited the Lord's Prayer as we bid our friend farewell."

Daniel, Lucy, Grace, Paul and the men from the funeral home complied as they recited the familiar prayer led in a strong, resonant voice by Tom Arthur.

CHAPTER 23

Soon after Ogden's burial, Lucy noticed Daniel becoming more restless and pointedly remote toward her. He would often fall asleep soon after their evening meal. He would then awaken, go to bed only to find he was unable to sleep. After tossing and turning for what seemed hours to Lucy, he would get out of bed and go downstairs. For the remainder of the night, whatever was bothering him caused sleep to be elusive. After several nights of this troubled routine, Lucy decided she should speak with him.

One morning, as she walked into the room where her husband was watching the morning news, she asked, "Dan, did you rest at all last night?"

"Not after I went up to bed. Couldn't seem to get back to sleep. Came down here, made coffee, read awhile and just sat here."

"What is it that's bothering you? I'm here if I can help you. It seems to me the bottom completely fell out of our relationship the day Ogden died. You know, you haven't spoken ten words to me over the past few weeks. Can we talk about whatever it is that has upset you? Are you worried about the estate? Is that it?"

"No, I'm not particularly worried about the damned estate. Tom Arthur will take care of all that. Sure, I want to see the thing brought to conclusion but I'm not concerned or worried about that."

"Have you been working on the story Ogden shared with you? I haven't noticed you going near the computer to re-write your notes, or for that matter, write anything. Are you having trouble getting back into that now that he's gone?"

"I'll work on whatever I decide to work on when I feel like it," he snapped, surprising Lucy with an unexpected and undeserved belligerent reaction. "What does all that matter to you, anyway? Give me a break, just lay off, will you? I just don't feel like going back over all that now. In the meantime, that matter is not for discussion or any of your business. Just forget about it, will you? And, just in case I forgot to mention it, you keep out of my files. Whatever Ogden told me is not for you to know. Do you understand what I'm telling you? You, Tom Arthur and the rest of world doesn't need to know what he told me. At least that's how it's going to be for now and maybe forever. I'm thinking of burning the entire, damned mess. Don't go looking around the house for my journal. I've hidden it where you will never find it and it's nowhere in the house."

"Well now, Dan, I'm sorry I brought that up. I didn't anticipate being attacked for simply asking an innocent question. I'm in no way telling you what to do with Ogden's story or anything else. You do what you feel is right."

"What else would I do? Do you think I need you to tell me that? Do you really think I need you or anybody else to tell me what I should do?"

"What is the matter with you? Well, no, of course I don't think that! I am trying to talk with you but all I'm getting from you is anger. I know I may be risking yet another assault from you, but please do not destroy those notes. Remember you signed a legal agreement with Ogden at Tom Arthur's office. I hope and pray you haven't already done anything like that. You know, that contract may be more binding than you think. This promise..." she hesitated before finishing what she wanted to say, "may prove difficult for you to disregard. I suggest you consult Tom Arthur before you go and do anything extreme.

"I just wanted you to know I'm here for you if you need to talk. You seem so tired. Why don't you try to rest while I start breakfast?" she added while wiping tears from her eyes as she stood and turned toward the kitchen.

"I don't want anything to eat. What in hell did you mean by 'this promise'? Sit back down over there for a minute. I'll probably come up with more than ten words, as you said, so make yourself comfortable. Since you're so anxious to talk, I have one question for you that I want you to think about before you answer," he stated as he looked away from where Lucy now sat. "I want to know why in hell you left that bottle of capsules on Ogden's nightstand before you took off for the grocery store."

"What? The bottle of...why...Daniel, I hope you don't think...No! You cannot believe I would have done that on purpose. Has that been bothering you to the point where you can't sleep? You must be thinking of me as some kind of very evil person. Someone who wanted that poor, sick man to die so we could somehow benefit. If that's what you have been thinking, you have been very wrong.

"Did you think I found his pistol and gave that to him, too? Why don't you have the pistol fingerprinted to see if I ever touched the thing? And his Bible? I'm sure my fingerprints would be on that if I had ever laid a hand on it. Go ahead and have them checked if you believe I did anything to hasten his death or make it easy for him to overdose himself. But, of course, you are probably imagining about right now, that I handled those two things while wearing gloves. See what I'm getting at? You've made it painfully clear that you can believe almost anything about me.

"Oh, this is way too much for me to withstand. I thought I had explained this to you before and thought you believed and understood what I told you. Look, I was in a hurry to go to the grocery store. After I gave Ogden his medication, I simply forgot to take the bottle back to the kitchen. That's all that happened and that's how it happened. I didn't design, I didn't plan or conceive an evil scheme to aid in the death of Ogden Royal. That's the truth of what happened. You decide for yourself if your wife is capable of euthanizing your friend.

"My conscience is clear on this. I regret making a mistake by leaving the medication within Ogden's reach. I've worried myself about that since it happened, but I'm innocent of what you imagine I did. Give me your hand," she said as she pleaded for contact that was pointedly rejected by Daniel as he still refused to look in her direction. "Well, if you refuse to hold my hand, at least make eye contact with me as I tell you, once again, the truth. I'm sorry I made a mistake but that's all I did.

"I'm hurt and shocked that you would even consider me capable of doing such a terrible thing," she continued angrily as she began sobbing softly and openly. "If you can't believe what I've said, then we have a major problem. You'll have to decide for yourself if your wife is the type person who would do such a deed. Is there nobody in the world you can trust?

"As for your journal, forget it! I'll not ask about that again. Don't worry about me trying to find the thing or even caring what you were told. As of a few minutes ago, I don't care what you do. Go ahead and quit this just like you've bailed out on so many other things in your life. When will you grow up? Hey look, you gave your word to Ogden, not to me. If you want to cut and run out on your promise, go ahead. I don't care. I've grown used to your starting something only to run into a problem, real or imagined, and quit before you completed what you had promised. I thought you said this time you wanted to achieve something meaningful and worthwhile. Well, for damned sure, if you don't fulfill your promise to yourself, that will not happen.

"If you weren't certain you would do all possible to get this job completed, you should have begged off earlier. Back home, we used to call people who habitually start things only to quit, 'half-asses.' Up until now, I never really wanted to think that about you, but you know, that's exactly what you sound like this morning.

"Time after time, I've stood by you when I didn't understand what you were doing. How many times have you started to do something, even a repair job around the house, only to make a great start then put it aside and quit? How many companies have trusted you, hired you, only to be left holding the bag just because things didn't go to your liking? If I didn't love you, I wouldn't, I could not have withstood all your self-hatred. That's just where all this is coming from, Dan. Pure and simple, you are so dissatisfied with what you have become you now loathe yourself. Now you are turning on me. If you are looking for someone to blame for whatever has brought you such misery, look at yourself. I am not your enemy.

"Now, out of my anger and hurt, I've said enough. You think it over and let me know what you decide, what you truly believe, by this evening. If you think you are going to mope around here with that hanged dog attitude without dealing with this issue, you are wrong. You are not going to give me the cold shoulder and clam-up so get those selfish ideas out of your mind. You are going to talk to me and your silly pouting about what you have imagined I did is going to stop. I hereby guarantee by all that's in my being, we will resolve this by tonight. It's time for you to decide just what you really believe about the woman you are married to.

"As I said, I know you are tired. I know this thing with Ogden has been stressful for you. I know all that but now you have created a more pressing problem. I'll stay out of your way today, and allow you to think. By this evening, I want your answer. If you continue to feel and believe as you do now, I will not stay in the same house with you. I will solve the problem for you while you sit on your hands and second guess your wife's character and motives." With that, Lucy went upstairs, showered, changed clothes, walked past Daniel on her way to the garage and drove away without speaking or offering to divulge where she was going.

When Lucy returned early that evening, she was surprised when she noticed Daniel had washed dishes and run the vacuum throughout the house. As she entered the room where he was sitting, she found him asleep. She was pleased his appearance had improved over what she had witnessed earlier that morning. He had evidently showered, shaved and changed into fresh clothing. When he heard her step out of the room, he stirred and asked, "Is that you, Lucy?"

"Yes, I'm back. Sorry if I woke you. Looks like you've been busy around here. Did you have a good nap?"

"What time is it now? I think I dozed off around two o'clock, or so. I did a few chores and took a bath. I came back down here, sat down and, well, you know the rest."

"Well, it's now after six, so you had a few hours of rest. Are you feeling better? Have you had anything to eat all day?" Lucy asked as she leaned against the doorway assessing Daniel's mood.

"I'm groggy…and starved! I didn't eat a bite all day," Daniel said as he stood and walked toward his wife. "Can you and will you ever forgive me for how I've been acting and for what I said to you this morning? I guess I just needed to hear you repeat what you told me the day Ogden died. I know I was wrong to imagine you would do such a thing. Sometimes this thing with Ogden weighs on my mind. I don't mean I'm overly concerned with any of the financial, legal wrangling because I'm not. All those details will be taken care of in due time.

"His story, Lucy, is bothering me. After we get the estate settled, I don't know how, or even if, I will be able to do anything more with that. I just don't know if I should take this any farther. Lucy, some of what he told me is very serious business. I want to share all that with you but, at the same time, I want to protect you from knowing all the details. Does that make sense to you? Do you understand the tightrope I feel I'm now walking?"

"Dan, you keep Ogden's story in a secure, hidden place for now. I don't have a clue as to what he told you. Judging from your troubled behavior, it must be something you consider too sensitive to share with anyone. If that's the case, I understand. I won't pry and try to get you to tell me what you are afraid might be harmful for me to know. I understand.

"I also want you to know you scared me this morning. I was hurt and angered by your words and by your accusation. Have you resolved that matter for yourself? Do you, even to the slightest degree, believe I left the medicine bottle there purposely? I want your honest answer now just as you asked for my honesty this morning."

"The matter is closed," Daniel replied in a plaintive voice. "I believe you did what you did because you were in a hurry to get what Ogden wanted. I never really believed anything to the contrary. I had conjured up one scenario and allowed my imagination to get the better of me. I apologize to you and I do love you dearly. I'm sorry for hurting you and for entertaining any doubt about you. Please forgive me."

"Dan, I spoke words this morning that were not meant to hurt you. What I said, I believe I had to say. What I said, I felt. I won't continue to be your enabler if you continue to gnaw at yourself for whatever is really bothering you. I know you believe you have been a failure in life. I know you are dissatisfied with your relationship with our children. I know all those things trouble you. Why dwell on the past? Why don't you look forward? You should try to be hopeful for a better future, a better relationship with the children. Why don't you reach out to them? If you will, I think you will be pleasantly surprised at their response. The kids don't dislike or hate you. They just don't understand you and probably feel you don't like them or want them around. I believe they sense you aren't pleased with yourself and that has affected your responsiveness and openness with them. Rather than disliking you, perhaps they feel you have rejected them.

"I don't know why you insist on comparing yourself to other people. You know, we've done very well for ourselves. Even without the money Ogden and Jane left us, we had plenty for a secure, satisfying life. We've always had everything we needed and most of what we wanted, when it came to material things. Maybe you should look around and notice all the people about our age who are far worse off than we are. You must quit looking backward. Whatever happened yesterday is over. Nobody can change anything about yesterday, wish and worry and walk the floor all night as they may. All anybody has is the present moment. Make the best of now and don't worry so much about tomorrow.

"I've spoken softly and kindly to you over the years. You obviously didn't hear or understand what I told you. I have myself to blame, as I think about it, because I stood by and watched you sink deeper and deeper into a self-imposed hell. You have passed a judgment on yourself that no man could withstand. You have never been able to forgive yourself so you have served a life sentence of self-torment. Only you can change all that for yourself. It all starts with you treating yourself a little more gently and little more lovingly. Does that thought scare you? Does the idea of forgiving yourself as you forgive other people repulse you? You know, psychologist tell us that it is impossible to love others if we hate ourselves. Does that thought seem reasonable to you?"

"Lucy, I know what you are saying is right. You have accurately described what I've done to myself. I see all that clearly now. I hate what I've done to our children. I wish I could have been a better father to them. Once again, when I think of the kids, I realize I'm caught between what I've become and what I should be. I know I can't change the past. With your help and support, I hope I can look back on the rest of my life, from today forward, with satisfaction. I'm willing to try; I want to make life better for you, our children and for myself."

"Okay, you understand what you've being doing to yourself. That's a start at taking the first positive step. As of this morning, I promise, for your benefit, and for our marriage, I will not continue to make the mistake of not speaking my mind. I'll help you if you will allow me to help. I want you to know, as I've told you many times over the years, I am with you. I'll stand by you until you drive me away.

"I'm telling you this now, as bitter as it may be for you to hear, that old, unworkable relationship is finished. We are beginning a new day, headed for a happier life that you have never allowed yourself to enjoy. Keep my sincere words in mind; listen to me this time, I am here to help you. Do you understand what I've told you?"

"Lucy, the truth stings as I listen to you explain how I have made you suffer and how you have been feeling, what you must have felt this morning. The truth is hurtful for me to hear, but you are right. I know I have problems. Try as I may to do and think otherwise, I always fall back into the same mean trap. I hear you, Lucy. I understand what I've been putting you through over the years. I'm sorry for the past but I vow, with your help, to begin a better life for both of us."

"As you said, and I believe you, the matter of how Ogden died is closed," she replied opening her arms offering an embrace that Daniel stood to accept. "I forgive you and I love you. Please talk to me when something is bothering you. Don't allow anything to get you into such a state. You should know by now, when something bothers you, it bothers me and I don't even have to know the source of your trouble. Always remember, as you struggle with what to do with Ogden's story, you have a friend who cares for you and loves you. Now," she smiled as they continued to embrace. "let's talk about getting you something to eat."

For Lucy the matter had been resolved. For Daniel, always the second-guesser, the self-doubter, the worrier, the matter, like so many others that had kept him bound to a miserable, limited past, remained an aggravating doubt in his mind. Much like Billy Merritt, Daniel had earned an unflattering nickname that he found difficult to forget. If his wife thought of him as a "half-ass," then perhaps she was correct in her assessment.

Dazed by Lucy's heartfelt summation of how she perceived him, Daniel vowed he would find a way to regain his wife's respect. He promised himself he would finish one task that would prove his determination to bring something to completion. Even if he never wrote another word, he knew, at last, what he must do to achieve his ultimate goal and that acknowledgement brought him a comfort he could not share with anyone. He also knew he must try to determine if Ogden had killed men named Merritt and Warren. He would begin by trying to find a name and an address that would lead him to someone he could contact who would reveal information that would refute or confirm Ogden's story.

CHAPTER 24

Daniel found a listing in the local telephone directory in the name of W. Merritt with an address in an area of Bloomington he knew indicated a neighborhood where individuals with limited financial means would likely reside. He had been all over Bloomington during his insurance career and recognized the address to be one of several small apartments built by the federal government to replace what had once been mostly plywood and cardboard hovels in a district known as The Hill.

Surrounding the newer units were small houses on crowded lots in various states of disrepair. Spouses and descendants of men and women who had worked long, hard years at menial jobs that had contributed to the wealth of those who lived in a different part of town now occupied those homes. Residents of The Hill were a hardened people who had endured in spite of circumstances. The topic of conversation inside those homes was not likely to revolve around how an investment portfolio was performing.

He decided he would have to visit W. Merritt to learn if that person could or would provide any information about Billy that might confirm or contradict Ogden's account. Whatever resulted from his investigation, whether Billy existed, had been a creation of Ogden's imagination or had in fact disappeared, it would not be necessary to pursue confirmation from the Warren family.

He decided he should take precaution and disguise himself. While not accustomed to such theater, he visited a local shop that specialized in costuming. There he found a moustache and a wig of different coloration than his natural hair. After he removed his rings and watch, he donned a wide-brimmed hat and an overcoat that might obscure his stature. He decided he would leave his eyeglasses in the car once he determined the location of the W. Merritt residence.

As he did not want his car in plain view of whoever might answer the door, he parked several blocks away and walked to the targeted apartment. Several older cars and trucks that were in various states of disrepair with a few displaying efforts of being tricked-out by cheap after-market accessories in an attempt to mimic the latest vehicle fad were parked on both sides of the street. Several groups of young men congregated in front of apartments with nothing to do except talk loudly and tease each other concerning their latest exploit or conquest, real or fabricated. As he approached, the loafers quieted and he could feel their eyes taking his measure as they assessed a stranger who might be invading their territory. Keeping one hand in his coat pocket, hoping to suggest he was armed and perhaps a police officer, he walked by without breaking pace or acknowledging their presence or their curiosity.

When he arrived at the door that displayed the listed apartment number, he noticed the front step and small front lawn appeared neat and orderly. A small cedar board someone had carved and painted with black lettering hung below the metal mailbox announced this was the residence of someone named "Merritt."

He had to knock twice before the door opened the three inches allowed by the security chain. "Yes, what do you want here?" asked a faint female voice from behind the door and out of his view.

"I'm sorry to have bothered you, ma'am, but are you Mrs. Merritt?"

"Maybe. But… who are you and what do you want here?"

"Ma'am, my name isn't important to you. I assure you I am here for a good reason and mean you no harm. Ma'am, do you know anything about a young man named Billy Merritt?"

"His name is William, just as was his father. He goes by Billy. Why are you asking me questions about my son?"

"Mrs. Merritt is your son at home, or do you know where I can find him?"

"What do you want with Billy? Why are you asking about my son? Why it any of your business…what gives you the right to come here asking me questions? Go away or I'll call the police," she replied as she began to shut the door.

"Wait just a second, ma'am. Well, this is kind of an old issue, Mrs. Merritt, but I owe your son a little money. I've been expecting to run into him somewhere around town but our paths haven't crossed in a long, long time. Wanted to pay him what I owe him and get the matter settled and off my mind. That's all I want. If you can tell me where he is or when he might return, I'll give him his money, what I owe him, and I'll be on my way and not bother you again."

"Why do you owe Billy money? What did he do for you that you owe him any money?"

"Billy worked for me out at my place several days one summer. He was supposed to return the next week for his pay but I never saw him again. Can you help me, Mrs. Merritt?"

Daniel stood quietly while she considered what he had said then she removed the chain and opened the door. "You can step inside for a minute, if you want," she volunteered as she pointed with her hand to where he should stand that indicated the extent of her hospitality.

He immediately noticed the cleanliness of the small home and the sparse furnishings. On a small table sat a picture of a stern-looking young man in a Marine uniform that he assumed to be Billy. He also noticed Mrs. Merritt, though small, bent and frail, was particular concerning her hair and appearance.

"Look, mister, you stop at my home saying you owe Billy some money. You didn't tell me your name. I figure you have reason for not wanting to volunteer any more information than necessary. I don't know anything about you, mister, but I know my son. If you say he earned whatever money you say you owe him, fine, I don't care but I know Billy wasn't one to work very long for anybody. It does not surprise me one bit that he failed to show up as he promised. I don't know anything about your business, but if Billy was in some kind of trouble or you have reason to lie to me, I don't care about that either. Look, I'm a tired old woman. I don't have much of anything, certainly not money, so if you are trying to scam me, it won't be worth your effort."

"No, Mrs. Merritt. I meant what I said. I owe your son a little money. If you'll tell me how I can reach him, I'll be on my way."

"The truth is, mister, I don't know where he might be. Billy left here one afternoon a long time ago and I haven't seen or heard a word from him or about him since. I reported his disappearance to the police but they haven't been able to be of any help. I just don't know what to tell you."

"Here," Daniel said as he pulled a sealed envelope from his coat pocket and handed it to a hesitant Mrs. Merritt. "I'm not able to keep looking for him and I need to get this settled and off my mind. There is a little over five-hundred dollars, cash, in this envelope. If he shows up, you can settle with him. In the meantime, well, you can use the money however you see fit."

"Thanks for your honesty. If Billy… ever…if he ever comes back here," she replied as tears began to fill her eyes, "I'll tell him about you and how you tried to find him."

"Thank you, Mrs. Merritt. I'll be on my way and not bother you any longer." With that, Daniel, without offering his hand, made a hasty retreat out the door and back to his car.

After he placed the key in the ignition and before starting the engine, he removed the wig and moustache. He sat transfixed and considered what he had just learned. He began to sweat and both his hands, now gripping the steering wheel, began to tremble. Whatever wishful reasoning he had invented and entertained that held hope Ogden had fabricated the deaths of two men was now pointless. Ogden had him told a true story unknowingly confirmed by a frail and tearful Mrs. Merritt. Ogden, he no longer doubted, had killed two young men one fall evening along the shoreline of Lake Monroe and that stark reality did not bring him peace.

CHAPTER 25

As Tom Arthur predicted, Ogden's estate proceeded through the system without contest or problem. After the real and personal property appraisals were completed and all assets totaled, Ogden's estate was valued at over six- million dollars.

When Lucy heard that large sum of money mentioned, her jaw dropped as she looked at Daniel with an amazed expression and said, "I figured Ogden and Jane were wealthy people, but I never dreamed they had accumulated such a fortune. How do you suppose they were able to save that kind of money and buy so much real estate?"

"Keep in mind they were very frugal people. I imagine Jane inherited some money from her folks and she did sell a prosperous downtown business. As for Ogden, well, he never spent money recklessly for any reason. Other than that," he paused as he considered how he would evade answering her question in a truthful manner, "I don't suppose it really matters to us."

Again, the lawyer had been correct when he estimated Daniel and Lucy would need almost all the proceeds from Ogden and Jane's life insurance policies to pay estate taxes and legal fees. The good news was they weren't forced to sell anything to raise money for those expenses. Their generous benefactors had made inheriting their considerable estate easy and painless.

They made an appointment with Tom to discuss selling some of the real estate property. They had decided they would sell their house and move into the much larger and nicer home on North Maple Grove Road. They also wanted to sell the rental units and to discuss moving money from Antigua into a brokerage account stateside. While moving such a large amount of money would entail some expense and expertise, they had decided they were not comfortable with the current arrangement.

They determined they would not sell the property in Minnesota until they had opportunity to visit the place themselves. They wondered if the cabin on Mayhew Lake might become an ideal setting for family vacations. If the property proved unsuitable for their needs, then an offer to sell would follow.

After the attorney offered his advice as how they could achieve their goals, he turned to Daniel and asked, "How are you doing with Ogden's story?"

"Not too well, I'm afraid. I haven't touched it since Ogden died. Tom, there's a part of what he told me that I'm not sure how to handle. Part of what worries me is how Ogden and Jane came into such a windfall of cash that came from a source outside their frugality and business skills," he confessed, jolting Lucy into rapt attention.

"The other part that really bothers me, well, I don't think I'm free to discuss with anyone, at this time, according to his wishes. I need your expertise concerning the contract you wrote for him concerning how and when I'm at liberty to proceed."

"Did they do anything you believe was illegal concerning their impressive accumulation of wealth? To be honest with you both, I was somewhat surprised when they contacted me about moving money offshore. That's not a request very many people in these parts make. Of course, the source of the money was none of my business. I didn't ask and they didn't volunteer any explanatory information."

"No, as far as I know they didn't do anything I consider illegal to get the money or anything else they owned. It was something that happened sometime after they transferred money to Antigua that's the real source of my problem."

"As for the contract between you and Ogden, it became void when he passed away. After all, it was so loosely written, as Ogden wanted, that there wasn't much there to bind you in the first place. It was a sort of 'can if you want to' agreement, if you recall. His story now belongs to you. I won't try to guess what he told you that is so bothersome for you. I don't know what you can do with the story, if anything. That's entirely your call now. As stipulated, it's now your property. You are no longer bound by Ogden or anyone else on that score."

"As our attorney, I suppose whatever I tell you will be held in confidence based on attorney-client privilege? Is that how this works, Tom?"

"Whatever you or Lucy need or want to tell me will not go outside this room. However, let me add, I will strongly advise you if I think there is anything that might create a legal problem for you down the road."

"No...nothing like that, Tom," Daniel stammered as his mind raced, "There is part of what Ogden told me that I don't think I should reveal as part of his story or in any other manner."

"Then don't include that part in whatever you choose to write concerning Ogden. Have you ever considered writing a fictionalized story? Who says you have to use actual names of the people involved? After all, I don't suppose you are thinking about writing a historical account with footnotes and references, are you?" Tom chuckled. "If you aren't comfortable writing the story exactly as told to you, write a story based on what you were told and avoid any possible conflict. Seems that might remedy your quandary. What do you think of that idea?"

"I like the sound of that. That might prove to be a workable solution. Guess I have been wrestling with trying to write something that accurately reflects the personality of the characters based on their actual words and deeds. Don't see why, now that you mention it, I couldn't take a few liberties and, hopefully, make the story even more interesting. Thanks, Tom. I'll give your suggestion more thought and see what I can put together."

As they drove away from Arthur's office, Lucy asked, "Did Tom's suggestion about writing a story without using actual names and places seem like an idea you might develop? Could his idea revolving around a fictional version be the answer to your dilemma?"

"I've been thinking about that from the moment he mentioned it. As Ogden told me, the story would become my property to do with as I see fit. I don't know just yet. I want to do something with that journal but just haven't been in the mood to get to work. You heard Tom when he said I'm free and clear to do as I see fit. That was a relief!

"I suppose I'm suffering from the same quandary Meriwether Lewis experienced when he returned from the Expedition. Lewis was obligated to write a report for President Jefferson but for a variety of reasons, he didn't fulfill that part of his promise. Not that my work is in the same league with what those men experienced but maybe that is a common problem once a mission is finished. You know, sort of a let down, anti-climatic? I think I'm just tired of the story for the time being. I'll get back to it soon and see what I can develop. Hey, when I do begin re-writing, you want to be my proofreader?" he smiled as he jiggled and rubbed Lucy's shoulder with his free hand.

"Sure thing, you know I'll do whatever you need done that will help you. I'd be pleased to be part of your writing if that's what you want. You know, I came to know Ogden fairly well myself. I'm available when you say the word." Lucy was relieved Daniel was now at least talking about the writing assignment that had once nearly consumed his total attention and energy. While pleased and somewhat relieved he had asked her to help, even in an off-handed manner, she felt any more discussion or questioning at that time might prove counter-productive.

If Daniel had meant what he said about getting back to work on his writing project, Lucy never noticed evidence of that taking place. Several weeks passed after their visit to Tom Arthur's office and he never mentioned the matter again. Day by day, he was slowly reverting into the same sullenness that had become so disturbing for Lucy before he accused her of contributing to Ogden's death.

She waited patiently and hoped her husband would retrieve the hidden notes and write something that would indicate he was motivated to complete what he had begun. As Lucy recalled later, it seemed as if she lived through those days by herself. She often wished Daniel had never met Ogden Royal.

When Lucy mentioned he might give the children a call, Daniel agreed that was a good idea but he never made the effort to contact them. While continuing to worry about his mental state, Lucy remained supportive and most other aspects of their life seemed to be going peacefully. She thought about asking Daniel to seek counseling but hesitated to broach a subject that might anger him or drive him into a deeper depression.

Contrary to what she had promised, Lucy decided to allow Daniel more time to sort out his feelings. Maybe, she consoled herself, one morning I'll be awakened by the clicking of his keyboard and the aroma of freshly-brewed coffee and all this turmoil will become a distant memory.

CHAPTER 26

Lucy didn't try to mask her surprise or reaction when Daniel suddenly and enthusiastically announced he planned to go see the property in Minnesota and intended to begin the trip in two days. He stated that Lucy was to remain at home and he would drive up by himself and take along the old Royal manual typewriter, as he wasn't sure how functional a computer would be in such a remote area. "Who knows," Daniel posed, "how much hassle will be involved with getting the electricity and telephone turned back on up there?" He explained he intended to begin putting Ogden's story into some comprehensible form and thought a change of scenery and seclusion would aid him in his effort.

Though she was puzzled at being summarily and unilaterally excluded from accompanying him on this trip, she determined it might be good for him to have time by himself. Perhaps that setting would rekindle excitement for his writing project that had eluded him thus far at home.

Lucy suggested Daniel drive the Mercedes to Minnesota as his car was old and unreliable. Daniel countered by answering his old car would do just fine. "I had the car inspected a few days ago," he sought to reassure her, "and I'm confident it is safe and roadworthy. Anyway," he added with a hint of mirth, "I'm not so sure I could handle your fancy machine! Don't concern yourself about what I'm driving. My old car should make the trip without any foreseeable problems. If not, well, I'll cross that bridge when I come to it."

Lucy wondered and then decided to ask him why he hadn't traded for a better, newer car now they could certainly afford to do so. She had noticed Daniel had not spent one dollar of the money from Ogden's estate. It was as if that money was off limits to him. When he ignored her question and changed the subject, she decided not to press the issue. She assumed his attitude toward using their wealth, even for necessities, would eventually change and she was willing to allow time for that to occur.

"Do you plan staying overnight with my family in Iowa?" Lucy asked intending to offer a suggestion. "If you want to do that, I'll give them a call and let them know you are coming. I'm sure it would be fine with them and, at the same time, give you a place to stay overnight and a break from driving."

"That won't be necessary. Don't want to impose or bother them. You know anything that rocks their boat, such as an overnight visit by the likes of me would twist their panties in a wad for days. No, I don't want to be the source of their constipation, even for one night. I plan to have a quick, pleasant trip, if you get my drift.

"I'll drive non-stop if I can. I want to get up there, look around and attend to my business. The quicker I get there and put a few ideas on paper, the quicker I'll be back. I realize it's a long trip but that will give me time to think and organize my thoughts before I sit down to do some writing. If I get overly tired, I'll stop somewhere and rest. I promise I won't drive impaired by lack of sleep. I'll call you while I'm on the road, just to keep you posted. Don't worry about me. I'll be just fine. I used to drive from Columbus, Georgia to Bloomington non-stop and I think I can still handle driving that far without much trouble.

"I'll get up there, as I said, have a look around and stay there for a few days. Oh, by the way, I should probably take sheets for the bed and a few bath towels and a blanket or two. I'll find a grocery store before I go to the cabin. Don't want to get up there and not have anything to eat. After all, it's thirty-some miles back to Grand Marais, so I'll need to plan my meals for the few days I'm there. Hey, this is sounding more like an adventure the more I think about it!"

Lucy was encouraged by Daniel's positive attitude, as he joyfully planned his brief getaway to an unfamiliar locale. "This may prove to be just what he needs," she thought as she sat on the bed and watched her husband pack a few clothes for a trip he was obviously anxious to begin.

Daniel was out of bed long before Lucy awoke the morning he left for Minnesota. "How long have you been up?" Lucy asked as she walked into the kitchen where Daniel was reading the newspaper and drinking coffee.

"Since before four o'clock. Woke up and rearin' to go! Anyway, I do want to get an early start. Get to the interstate before the school buses clog the roads. From here to Interstate 74 can be like driving in a parade if slowed by school and rush hour traffic. Of course, as we've experienced each time we've driven across Illinois, there is always mile after mile of aggravating roadwork to hinder traffic. I still say they have the wrong people building their roads. Maybe they should hire a few civil engineers from Purdue who know what they are doing. Oh well, my ranting about constant road repair on I-74 isn't going to change anything. Guess the politicians in Illinois have to keep their political contributors happy and one way to insure that happens is to approve sub-par work and materials that require constant patching.

"I figure it's a little over nine-hundred miles to Grand Marais and about another thirty miles up to the cabin. I called the electric and telephone companies up there a couple of days ago, gave them a credit card number and asked them to get the power and telephone turned on before I get there. I'll stop by their offices before I go on up to the cabin just to make sure and ask about the exact location of the property. If the power isn't on, I'll stay in motel and check again the next day. Who knows how responsive and dependable they will be at the request of a total stranger? Well, I'm about to find out, I suppose."

"Seems you've been busy getting everything you can think of in line for your visit. That's good. I'm glad you thought of doing that. Let me fix you a good breakfast before you take off. What would you like?"

"Just some toast and a piece or two of fruit. This is a bit earlier than we usually eat and I'm not very hungry. I'll stop somewhere for a better breakfast later this morning. Get some coffee and take a break from driving. I'll probably stop after I've been on the interstate for a few miles. I'm thinking maybe I'll wait until I get to Champaign or Bloomington, Illinois. Give me something to look forward to and by that time, I'm sure, I'll need to get out and stretch."

Soon after he finished a light breakfast, Lucy helped him carry two pieces of luggage and the old typewriter to his car. As they stood in the garage, Daniel held Lucy close and reiterated his love for her. After promising to keep occasional telephone contact as he progressed toward his destination, he backed his car out of the garage and began what he had referred to as an adventure.

Daniel didn't telephone Lucy until after he was on Interstate 35-West, making his way out of Minneapolis. By the time he called, Lucy was becoming concerned, as she had been ked to expect he would keep in closer contact throughout his journey. During that seemingly endless day and evening, she had wondered several times if she should call to check on him but decided the interruption might be distracting if not unwelcome.

"The traffic isn't too heavy here at this time of day," he sounded pleased. "Guess I hit this town about right to avoid that hassle. Lucy, I think I'll stay the rest of tonight in Two Harbors. I have a few more hours of driving to get to Duluth then I'll take Highway 61 that runs along Lake Superior for a few miles before I stop at a motel. Grand Marais is about two or three hours north of Two Harbors, so I think I'll pull in there and rest. I can't accomplish anything if I arrive in Grand Marais at three or four o'clock tomorrow morning. I think the best thing I can do is get some rest. I won't call you again tonight as it will be very late when I stop. I'll call you tomorrow after I get into Grand Marais and check on the status of the utilities."

"Glad you finally called. I've been expecting to hear from you. I have been worried about you all day. What happened? Have you had a good trip so far? How has the weather been today?"

"No problems on the road. The weather has been nice and clear. Not much different, so far, than what is was when I left home this morning. I didn't call because I didn't want to bother you. Thought about it a few times but got to thinking about one thing then another. You know how absent-minded I can be when I get to thinking about what I'm going to write. Well, that's been the case today. I'm fine but looking forward to getting out of this car and stretching my legs, that's for sure."

He had been truthful when he stated he had been thinking. He had been less than honest when he led Lucy to believe he had been thinking about what he would write.

"Well, it looks like I'm about out of Minneapolis, thankfully, and into even lighter traffic. Tell you what, I'll call you again tomorrow around ten or eleven, or so. Give you a report on how my night went and what Grand Marais looks like. Are you doing alright?"

"I'm good but I miss you. You have a good night and drive carefully. I'll be expecting to hear from you sometime midday tomorrow. Love you."

"You take care of yourself and make sure the house is secure. Don't want anybody paying you an unwelcome, unexpected visit. Talk with you tomorrow."

As he had promised, Daniel called Lucy the next day after he stopped to make sure the utilities were in service. The clerk at the telephone office, he pointedly told his wife, had told him landline service throughout the Gunflint Trail area, the location of Mayhew Lake, was, at best, unpredictable and cell phones were useless. He volunteered he would call her when he arrived at the cabin if that was possible. If not, even if he had to drive back into town, he would call home no later than tomorrow at about the same time.

He sounded eager to find a grocery store and then drive up the Trail to the cabin. Lucy was relieved he had spoken in a more relaxed and purposeful manner than she had heard for a long time.

While shopping for the grocery items he anticipated he needed, he looked around the store for an alcoholic beverage isle. Not finding what he wanted, he asked the cashier if they sold liquor. "You'll not find any private businesses selling those products. Cook

County restricts the sale of alcohol. There's just one place that sells beer, wine and such. The county liquor store is downtown, right around the corner from the visitor's welcome center. You can't miss it if you park near the center," she directed.

Once he found the beverage store and went inside, he browsed the shelves to see if a particular brand of whiskey was available. Daniel was not a drinker so he did not hold any preference for one intoxicating drink over another. He had heard the particular label he was looking for was "pleasant" and that was the sole basis for his search. While he didn't know what he wanted to drink, he believed what he planned to accomplish required something that packed a stronger punch than coffee.

As he stood at the counter to pay for the whiskey, a talkative local noticed the cell phone hanging from his belt. "Don't know where yer headed, but that device won't likely be much good very far out of town," the stranger volunteered, offering to converse.

Daniel answered, "Not too far," in a terse and non-committal manner as he completed his purchase and promptly left the store.

"I think you'll be pleasantly surprised when you see this place," was his greeting when Lucy answered the telephone early that same afternoon. "I've been here almost two hours and I've been throughout the cabin, which isn't an accurate term for this place. Three bedrooms, a very nice kitchen, dining area, a living room with a fireplace that is massive, well, you'll just have to see it for yourself. The lake is big and looks very nice. Ogden had a small boat dock built just a few years ago by the looks of it. Out in the storage building, I found a flat bottom fishing boat and a canoe. Motor boats aren't allowed on this lake and I understand why. Who needs all that noise and pollution in these waters?"

"Glad to hear you like the place and that it is so nice. I'll bet the place needs a good cleaning. When was the last time Ogden and Jane were there?"

"I don't know. Ogden never said much about it. I imagine it's been at least four or five years since they were up here. With Ogden being so ill, I doubt they made this trip since all that started. Oh sure, there is a little dust here and there but all the furniture had been covered. I'll go over a few things, open the windows to allow some fresh air in, you know, make it as comfortable as it needs to be for a brief visit. You know, Lucy, I think you and the kids will love it up here. This is a different world than what they have ever experienced. People up here seem independent, so self-sufficient. A tougher breed of folks, it seems to me."

"I hope you will enjoy being there with us as well," Lucy added. We can all have a good time together, don't you think?

"Sure, I didn't mean I wouldn't like being here. I just meant I think this will be a place where you and the kids will enjoy coming and being together."

"Well, you sure seem pleased with the place. That's good. I'm looking forward to when we both can spend some time up there. When you get back home, it might be nice if you called the kids and told them about the cabin. Maybe we could arrange a family vacation and all of us go up there for a week or so. What do you think of that possibility?"

"When I get back, we'll see what everyone wants to do. Probably be next to impossible for everyone to agree on a time to come up here. Seems as though they keep so busy they don't have much time for the likes of me. You are the one who has maintained a closer relationship than what I could ever manage. Maybe you should be the one to mention this to them. Oh well, we don't have to decide that right now. Maybe when they hear it won't cost them much, they'll be more agreeable."

Lucy detected Daniel's tone had suddenly become negative and defensive when she mentioned contacting the children. He had become contemplative, measured and sounded almost bitter. Why did he harbor such feelings about his own children? Why did he fear they would reject him? Did he feel he didn't deserve their respect? Whatever it was, she began to worry he had capitulated to his old mode of self-flagellation and self-loathing.

"I'm sure they'll all be happy to visit that area with us. You sure sound impressed by what you've seen so far," she tried to turn the conversation toward a happier, positive point.

"Don't be concerned if you should call here and not be able to get through. Like I said, Mayhew Lake is about 34 miles from downtown. The cabin sets off the main road about another half-mile. The gravel road around the lake is lined by trees with overhanging limbs that could rip down telephone lines. Cell service is non-existent, so don't bother with that," he replied somewhat sternly while changing the subject.

"You said you figured that would be the case. I'll put the new number on my contact list and use that instead," she agreed.

"As I mentioned before, the weather and old, poorly maintained telephone lines often interrupt service in this area. If that should happen, don't worry yourself. It's part of the way of life here and can be expected on a frequent basis. I'll not drive down to Grand Marais everyday but I'll make a special trip if I don't hear from you after a day or two," he answered sidestepping Lucy's attempt to turn their conversation toward a subject he did not want to pursue.

"Dan, are you alright? All of a sudden you don't sound so happy, so up-beat. Remember, you can tell me anything that bothers you. Talk to me…"

"Lucy, I'm fine," he interrupted. I have never been better. I don't know what you are talking about or how I may sound to you. I don't need to discuss anything with you or anyone else. I'm fine. Listen, I need to get a few things from the car and fix a little something to eat. I want to look over my notes this evening and get a little work done. Talk to you again… soon."

With that brusque summation, he ended the conversation with his wife without allowing a response or by taking a few moments to wish her a pleasant evening. Lucy was shocked by the capricious turn of his mood and became shaken that her husband didn't sound well. She regretted mentioning the children as that seemed to be the point where the conversation became strained and difficult for him.

Lucy called the cabin the next afternoon but Daniel didn't answer. She thought he was probably outside looking over the lake or perhaps he was on his way into town for some forgotten need. When she called the second day, she heard a busy signal. She remembered what he had told her concerning the unreliable telephone service and thought he should be calling the next day. She tried again the third day without success and began to worry. "If he doesn't call here tomorrow," she told herself, "I'll call up there to see if I can get someone to check on him."

CHAPTER 27

He ignored each ring of the telephone because he knew it was his wife trying to contact him. In an attempt to play along with the probability of failing phone lines, he had disconnected the phone jack for a few hours each day. He decided he wouldn't answer her calls as he was deep in thought and occupied but not with the stated purpose of his trip to the cabin. "What she doesn't know won't hurt her and what she needs to know about her half-assed husband, she'll find out soon enough," he spoke aloud to himself.

As the fourth day passed without word from Daniel, Lucy decided she would call someone in the area who would answer her call. A quick check on the internet gave her the telephone number of the Cook County Sheriff's office located in Grand Marais. "This will likely put him into a rage, but I'm going to find out what's going on up there," Lucy thought. "If he had done as he promised, I wouldn't be sitting here worried out of my mind. If he had called me, this wouldn't have been necessary. I hope a visit from the local sheriff does piss the selfish bastard off. Maybe that will wake him up and cause him to finally realize he is loved, that I care for him and I depend on him."

After the telephone rang twice, a clipped Minnesotan voice answered, "Cook County Sheriff's office, this is Sheriff Johnson. How kin I help ya?"

After she identified herself, explained her situation and asked if someone from the office could stop at the cabin, the Sheriff replied, "Well, ma'am, we are a small department here and we don't drive the Trail twice a day, unless there's an emergency, ya know. Already made our daily trip up and around Seagull Lake, which is practically at the end of the trail and about sixty miles north of town. Tell ya what, if you'll tell me which cabin your husband is staying in, I'll stop by there on my way through there tomorrow."

"The cabin is on Mayhew Lake. The property now belongs to us but it was once owned by Ogden and Jane Royal, if that helps you."

"Yah, you bet, that certainly does help. Know exactly the cabin you're talking about. Hey, you say you bought it from Ogden Royal? How are those folks doin' these days? As far as I know, they haven't been up here for several years."

"I'm sorry to tell you that Mrs. Royal was killed in an auto accident and Mr. Royal passed away a few months ago. He suffered through a lingering illness that made it difficult for him to travel far from home. Did you know them well?"

"Well, I'm very sorry to hear 'dat. I didn't know either of them real well, no, but I know she was a fine lady and he was a good man. They came up here several years ago, long before they bought the place on the lake, to visit my folks. You see, my older brother was in Vietnam and was in Ogden's unit. Neil carried the radio for him. Ogden was shot up pretty badly over there and my brother, well, he didn't survive. Ogden and his wife made a special effort to come up here so Ogden could tell my parents how much he had admired Neil. Ma and Pa appreciated his thoughtfulness and kindness. He certainly didn't have to do what he did for my parents. Ogden Royal was a special man and a true gentleman in my book."

"My husband and I admired Ogden and Jane and held them both in high regard. Sheriff, I'm very worried about my husband. I've been trying to call him for days without answer. He told me he would call home if I wasn't able to get through to him.

That was four days ago. I don't mean to be a bother to you, but I'm sure you can appreciate my concern."

"No bother, Mrs. Tyler. That's part of my responsibility. We get this type of request more than you might think. I'll drive up there tomorrow sometime and pay your husband a visit. He's probably out on the lake rowing around in a canoe and having the time of his life. I'll make sure he gets your message. If we can't call you from the cabin, I'll call you when I get back here to the office. Now you just relax and don't worry. Rest assured I'll do as I say. Now, you try to have a restful evening and leave this to me. Again, I'm really sorry to hear about Mr. and Mrs. Royal."

"Thank you, Sheriff. You have been very considerate and helpful. I'll keep my cell phone close by all day tomorrow waiting to hear something. Thanks again. Good bye.

Just as she ended her with Sheriff Johnson, the telephone rang. "Daniel? Where have you…"

"No, Mom, this is Danny," the caller interrupted. "Listen, where is Dad? He called here a few minutes ago and he sounded different. Said he just wanted to say hello and tell me he loves me. Said he was sorry for the way things have become between us and he wanted me to know he wishes he could have been a better father. What's this all about, Mom?"

"Oh, Danny, I'm so glad you called! I don't know what all is going on with your dad. Since his friend Ogden Royal died, he has been going through an awful time. He's up in northern Minnesota, near Grand Marais, at the cabin Ogden left us. He told me he was going up there to look the place over, and do some writing. He promised he would keep close contact and let me know how he's doing. The last time I spoke with him was almost four days ago. I just got off the phone with the county sheriff. I called there to see if someone would drive to the cabin and see if everything is all right. Danny, I'm worried sick about him. I don't know what else I can do until I hear from Daniel, or the sheriff, tomorrow."

"Mom, you know how he can be. I admit I was surprised when he called. That's not like him to call for any reason, let alone to say he loves me and that he is sorry for our relationship, or for anything else. You know, for a person who writes, he sure finds it difficult to share feelings with people who love him."

"I know, Danny. I also know he dearly loves each of you kids. You do believe that, don't you? He's a strange person, in many ways. I know he often thinks of you and he used to laugh about some of the things you, Lucinda and John did when you were small. I know he doesn't love himself and, at times, I wonder if he has ever loved me, but you kids are a different matter to him.

"Mom, I think all his confused feelings began when we were kids in school. I remember those nights when he would drill, drill and drill some more until we could instantly answer a question that might come up on a test. You know, he was a tough taskmaster when it came to our schoolwork. At the time, I thought he was just being mean, but then I was thinking as a child. To paraphrase the Bible, 'When I was a child I thought as a child.' Well, now I'm glad the old man insisted we perform to our abilities in school. Look at us now. Each of us has become successful in our chosen professions. Lucinda has a thriving medical practice and John is becoming an excellent defense attorney in northern Indiana. As for me, I'm very happy to be teaching chemistry at Purdue University. Not a bad result, three for three, if you ask me."

"Have either of you ever told him what you just told me?"

"No, well, I know I haven't, but I should have. You know he can be difficult to talk to sometimes. He always seems so preoccupied. There always seems to be something on his mind that will not allow him to sit down and relax. He makes it difficult to get close to him. Believe me, I wish we could all share how we feel toward each other."

"Do you understand why he was so intent that all you kids received a solid education? You know, your father grew up very poor and his parents, loving though they were, didn't emphasize the importance of education. As a result, your dad skated through high school never really making an honest effort. He suffered from that inadequate background throughout his academic life. When he went to college, he was lost. He had to work hard just to get through. He wanted better, far better, for his children. He wanted you kids to achieve what was beyond his ability. That's why he was so demanding. He didn't intend to drive you kids away from him or to be mean to you. He wanted to make sure each of you was prepared for whatever you might chose to do. As you said, each of you benefited from his rigorous discipline. You know, he's very proud of his children.

"He doesn't often show how he really feels about anything, but his love for you should not be questioned. For some reason I haven't been able to fathom, he believes he was a terrible father, a failure as a parent, as a husband and as a provider. Whatever he expected from himself, he did not, could not, attain.

"Danny, your father is a loner. You know, the only person he considered a friend was Ogden Royal. Throughout all the years he worked with and around other people, he never spent more than five minutes with any of them outside work other than Ogden. He was miserable dealing with people in business. Look at what happened when he began writing for the newspaper. When he was writing on a regular basis, he was a different man. He became more contented and pleased with himself as never before. When that creative, studious outlet ended, he tried to cope with the letdown. I was thrilled when he told me Ogden had asked him to do some writing for him. Once again, that interaction brought him back to having a meaningful purpose. It seems Ogden's death was a letdown that he hasn't been able to overcome.

"Danny, your father has led a very unhappy, unfulfilled life, in his own estimation. My words and encouragement to the contrary have not lessened his punishing self-image. He just cannot seem to put the past to rest. I'm worried about him and don't know what to do."

"Listen, I'm much closer to his location than you. I'm going to head up there tonight. I should be there sometime early tomorrow afternoon. If you'll give me a few more details concerning the exact location, I'll use my GPS and get started. Did he drive his old car up there? What's the name of the lake where the cabin is located?"

"Danny, I think you should go to your father but be careful. You might want to stop by the Sheriff Johnson's office on your way to the cabin. Just tell him who you are and that you are looking for a cabin on Mayhew Lake that belonged to Ogden Royal. That way, somebody there will be able to give you good directions. From what Daniel told me, the property is over thirty miles north of Grand Marais. He did drive the old car up there, so you can look for that when you arrive. That's going to be a long drive even for you, Danny. Are you sure you want to make the trip alone?"

"Mom, I'm getting ready to leave as we speak. You know, Lucinda and John aren't too far from me. I'll call them to see if they can make the trip with me. I imagine Dad has called them as well, so my call shouldn't be too much of a shock. Mom, you relax and take it easy. I'll call you as we get this together. I'll let you know if Lucinda and John make the trip with me. I'll keep you posted but I won't call you after bedtime. Is that alright?"

"Yes. I understand. All three of you kids have been wonderful children. Maybe this crisis will be the beginning of a better relationship for all of us. At least, that's my hope. I love you. Danny, please take care and be careful."

After she concluded that conversation with her eldest child, Lucy dialed the number at the cabin. She began to sob as she counted the beeping of the busy signal and acknowledged her attempts to contact Daniel were, once again, futile.

A few minutes later John, then Lucinda, called their mother. They both shared the same information with her Danny had recounted. Both were concerned and didn't know what they should do. Lucy told them to expect a call from their brother who was preparing to drive to Minnesota. Both children said they would arrange their weekend schedules and be ready when he called. Lucy hoped, as they traveled that long road together, they would share their experiences and feelings concerning their father. Perhaps their collective insights and memories would lead them to more fully appreciate and realize how much he loved them.

CHAPTER 28

Daniel had been alone at the cabin for four days and hadn't touched the journal he said he intended to begin re-writing during the time he was away from home. The morning after Danny and his other two children had departed for Minnesota, he stood near an old Adirondack chair and table down by the lake that hadn't been moved or used for several years. He had brought along the notes he had hand-written for Ogden. He surveyed the shoreline as he looked for pieces of dry kindling he could gather in order to start a small fire. He had decided the first step he would take to resolve his misery.

After he had collected a handful of twigs and a few small branches sufficient for his purpose, he returned and cleared leaves and needles from the old chair and table. Before he sat down, he removed the bottle of capsules that bore the name of Ogden Royal from one jacket pocket and sat it on the small wooden table. For good measure, he had brought along Ogden's 9mm pistol loaded with a magazine of ammunition. A 375ml bottle of Bushmills Irish whiskey and a bottle of water completed what he assumed he would need to redeem himself from being a "half-ass" in Lucy's eyes. As he studied the container of capsules, he twisted the cap off the bottle of whiskey, took a quick sip and then, discovering the golden-colored liquid to his liking, returned the bottle to his mouth for a prolonged, guzzling drink.

"Well, Lucy," he thought to himself, "This will be for you. I'll complete one task in my miserable life and that will give you reason to be real proud of me or forget about me altogether. At least you won't have to put up with a half-ass any longer. You won't have to worry about me and all my problems after this morning. It will be a new beginning for you, Lucy, that's for sure.

"My dear Lucy you sure as hell deserved a whole lot better than what I was able to provide. The kids, well...I at least told each of them I love, or loved, them. They should all be relieved at not having to tiptoe around their old man whenever they decide to visit you. Hell, they can all come up here when they want and enjoy themselves without having to waste their precious time worrying about what I think."

He replaced the cap on the bottle, stood and started to walk toward where he planned to build a fire. "I'll take care of Ogden's story before I take care of Lucy's problem," he thought just as a faint rustling from down near the lake diverted his attention.

"Hello there! How's fishin' this mornin'?" echoed a man's voice far enough away from an indiscernible location along the aspen and pine tree-lined lakeshore that prevented Daniel from detecting who was calling out to him.

Within moments, an angular older man came into view. He was wearing blue jeans rolled up two turns above his well-worn boots and a long-sleeved black and red-checkered flannel shirt. A sweat-stained baseball cap was haphazardly perched on his head. In one hand he carried a walking stick and in the other, a banana.

As the stranger made his way toward Daniel, he smiled and volunteered, "Don't believe I have ever saw ya' around these parts before. Last person who stayed in this place was old Ogden. Would ya be his son?"

"No relation, I'm afraid. My wife and I took the place over from Ogden after he died a few months ago. First time I've ever been up here," he explained thinking how he could delay and distract the unexpected visitor long enough to get the bottle of capsules and pistol off the table and out of sight.

"Well, ya know, sorry to hear that about Ogden. Got to know him over the years when they would come up for a few days. Wasn't a talkative sort, that's for sure, but he was good company, in my book. Say, whatever you were doing, don't let me stop ya. I see you were fixin' to build yourself a fire? Wanna be careful with fire in these parts. Yes sir, fire is a big problem once out of control, as you can imagine.

"I was just walking around the lake this morning looking at the wildlife, ya know? Love to be outdoors and saw you standin' and workin' around here and thought I'd introduce myself so if ya see me again you won't think I'm some sort of prowler," the stranger laughed easily as he perched himself on a nearby stump.

"My name is Tom Grillo, almost forgot to tell ya that. My place is about twelve miles south of here near Lullaby Creek. Fisherman, hunter, trapper and guide. That's about all I've ever done since I came back here from Korea in 1952. Some will probably tell ya I never amounted to much but they'd be wrong. If enjoying life and loving what ya do to pay your bills could be counted for anything, I'd say I've been mighty fortunate. As I read somewhere once, if you find something ya really like doing, you'll never go to work another day of your life. Well, that's pretty darned close to describing my life, not meaning to sound boastful. The way I live and work doesn't pay much, but I'm happy all the same. How have things been going for…you," Tom asked as his eyes darted to the bottle of capsules, then to the pistol, then to the whiskey then back to Daniel with a piercing look of concern.

"Didn't mean to be rude and not introduce myself, Mr. Grillo." Daniel offered his hand as he attempted to ignore the question he didn't want to answer while he tried to remain between the old man and the table. "I'm Daniel Tyler. My wife and I live near Bloomington, down in Indiana and I once worked with Ogden at an insurance agency. That's where we met. Over the years, we each went our separate way but we managed to remain friends. After Jane and Ogden passed away, we inherited this place. We decided not to be in a hurry to sell, at least until we had a chance to look it over."

"Call me Tom, no need for formality here. Sorry to hear they're both gone, that's for sure. Both were mighty fine folks. Well, if you decide to keep this place, we'll get to know each other better. Ya sure would be welcome to go on a walk with me sometime. No telling what we might see. Birds of all sorts migrate here and some species stay around through the winter months. Just saw an eagle pick a coot off the water a few minutes ago. Moose are seen in this area but they are reclusive creatures that prefer their own company. You have to walk lightly or you'll never see a moose, at least for any length of time. We'd have to get a little bit north of here, up toward Seagull Lake, if you're lookin' to see a bear or a wolf. Well, ya can keep my offer in mind if that should ever strike your fancy. I'm in and around one lake or another almost daily. If I'm not guidin', I'm outdoors doing somethin'.

"So, how was the insurance business for ya? Did you enjoy that line of work?" the old man insisted on prolonging the conversation while ignoring Daniel's obvious nervousness and discomfort.

"Enjoy?" he blurted out, the strong drink taking effect. "No, I never enjoyed that line of work or any other work that involved dealing with people. I earned a decent living, I'll say that much. Unfortunately, for my family as well as for me, I went to a job each day that I never enjoyed. I never seemed to find work that was a perfect fit for me. As I sit here this morning, Tom, I'd say life, work, and family have all pretty much kicked my ass."

"Oh, yah, so that was your problem. That's a lofty goal, ya know, seeking the perfect in your work, in yourself or in anything or anybody else. Well, ya know what happened to the only person who walked this earth who was truly perfect, don't ya? Well, of course, he did and said things that riled the powers of his time. After they beat him for good measure, they took that fella out of town and nailed him to a cross. Nah, that perfection goal isn't realistic for you or anyone else. It seems to me that you have been lookin' for something far beyond humanity to achieve.

"Well, you know, you are still a relatively young man. Are you retired?" the old man persisted. "You must have done something, sometime, you enjoyed. You don't appear to be showing much wear and tear. Ah, ya know if we're allowed another day, the way I see it, we can always hope for a better tomorrow."

"Yes, I am retired. You know, Tom, I felt I had a purpose when I was in the Army. When I came home from Vietnam, I figured I would continue to enjoy life and accomplish something worthwhile. Something I could look back on, feel some sense of accomplishment and maybe even a little pride. One mistake, one bad decision followed by another has taken its toll on me. For some reason, I look back on what I've done with my life and can't seem to make much sense of it or forgive myself for my failures. I suppose we all get, in the end, what we deserve. I've brought misery to my wife and children…and myself. I know that."

"You're too darned old to go back into the Army," Tom chuckled. "So has there been anything else that you enjoyed doing? If you have a wife and kids who love you, I'd say you are a lucky man and that's a wonderful accomplishment. I've never had a wife, a partner, and I've often wished I had. I keep busy, and overall I'm happy, but it gets lonely sometimes, as ya might imagine."

"There have been times when I enjoyed life. Sure, my wife, Lucy, and our three children have been a blessing to me in many ways. Now it seems to me, we've all grown apart. Conflicting expectations and all that sometimes makes it tough for us to understand each other. During the time I was writing a column for a local newspaper, well, I look back at that and admit that was a good time for me. If I could get back to writing, I believe, like you, I would never go to work again."

"Then, Daniel, that's your answer," Tom stated kindly as he once again surveyed the capsules, pistol and half-empty whiskey bottle sitting nearby.

"I don't know, and won't ask, what you were planning to do when I called out and came up here to speak with you. I see you have a bottle of pills, a pistol and most of a jug of whiskey on the table," Tom summarized. "Looks like you are prepared for a multitude of possibilities. As I said, none of my business and I won't interfere but I hope we can go for that walk sometime… if you decide to stick around. There's a lot of beauty and wonder in this old world if you care to take it all in, that's for sure. Make the most of your day, Daniel Tyler. Keep at it and you'll find your way.

"Oh, by the way, before I head off to find a place to sit and eat this banana and leave ya alone, have ya heard the one about the Norwegian who decided he would drown himself by sticking his head in a wash tub filled with water? When his brother saw what he was about to do, the brother asked, 'Vell, if yer gonna do 'er, why don't ya yust shoot

116

yerself? That would be lots quicker.' 'Ya, yer right 'bout that,' came the reply, 'but doin' 'er this way I'll have time to stop if I change my mind.'"

"Daniel Tyler, as I continue my walk along this beautiful lake, I'll pray for you and hope you find the answers you are seeking." Then Tom Grillo turned toward Daniel and added softly, "Ya know, ya still have time to change your mind." With that, the old man walked briskly toward the lake and never looked back to where Daniel sat, dumbfounded and slumped on the chair.

As his three children were speeding northbound toward the cabin on Gunflint Trail, rushing to be with their father, his wife sat at home anguishing, wishing and praying she would hear from someone. Aside from all her hopes, Lucy couldn't escape the feeling that something had gone wrong with Daniel. She acknowledged his discontent and self-hatred had come to the point where he would either surrender or triumph. The fleeting thought of Daniel yielding to his doubts and demons then harming himself churned a burden she did not want to entertain.

Once again, she dialed the number to the cabin. She sat transfixed as ring after ring went without answer. "Oh," she began to sob, "Why did I ever believe him when he hatched up this scheme to go up there by himself? I should have known he hadn't changed. I should never have allowed myself to believe he could pull himself out of his sickness that quickly or easily."

Daniel, unaware his children were now in the same county where he sat deciding his own fate, took another long swallow of the whiskey that seemed to bring clarity and comfort as he remembered what Tom Grillo had said. "I don't think the old guy would have said a word...or made a move...if I had placed the pistol to my head as he stood there and watched me...kill myself. I still have time...the old man said. Maybe I do have time to make amends with my wife... and children and get on with my life. Maybe I have time to accomplish...something that makes sense...to me. Then, maybe I'm another of God's creations predestined to wither...rot...fail...to yield goodness. Maybe I'm all out...of...out of...time. Maybe it is...it's time...to finish something I started. I'm sure Lucy and the kids would be...somehow...pleased with a different turn of events. Hell...the old man reminded me of Ogden, talking the way he did about trying to be perfect...and all," as his thoughts became more fragmented as the alcohol intensified its powerful, numbing effect.

"Ogden Royal," he thought as he brought the bottle to his lips for another drink, "said he wanted me to do... two things for him. Well, I've written down what he wanted to say. That was the first item on his damned list. Why in hell didn't he come out and tell what the second part of his plan involved? Oh, I remember, Ogden was too damned secretive to volunteer anything willingly. Was that what he meant when...he spoke of supporting certain charities and giving money to Merritt and Warren's parents?

"Maybe the second part of what Ogden had in mind was for me to take his story to the police...but no, he didn't know, at the time, he would lose Jane before his own death. No! He wouldn't have wanted Jane entangled with a police investigation of two murders and...have to explain all that money. Whatever he had in mind, he did say his story would be mine to do with as I saw fit. That's just what I'll do, Ogden, old friend...as I see fit," while remembering his plan to build a fire.

At that moment, his attention became riveted on the pistol and then on the bottle of capsules sitting on the table within his reach. As he brought the whiskey bottle to his mouth for another long, draining drink, he reclined on the old chair and began to relax. He imagined an immediate and welcome relief from a life of disappointment and his veil of tears if he could muster enough courage to swallow several of the capsules or pull the trigger.

CHAPTER 29

As he riveted his attention on the pistol and then the bottle of capsules, the whiskey hammered his brain and brought a quick and fitful sleep. In his stupor, he was agitated by confused and foggy thoughts while his body refused to be comforted as he twisted and turned from side to side. Effects of alcohol, fortified by mental exhaustion slowly began to uncover truths he had fought long and hard to ignore. While he tossed and turned, he was frightened, troubled, drunk and then, suddenly, it seemed, peaceful. Sane and calming dreams began to permeate his mind and whispered a clarity that surpassed his understanding. The rapid consumption of alcohol, the crutch intended to steel him to do what he thought he must, had subverted his plan by lulling him to sleep and then brought startling realizations he had not expected.

As he slept, he began to see himself as he was and for the man he had become. His shame, his weakness, his self-hatred, his inability to forgive appeared to him in large white letters affixed to brightly colored pennants. Those bitter messages waved and snapped in the wind and hung from sturdy, tall poles that commanded his attention and were captivating in their confirmation of his failure.

Small, comparably insignificant banners, discernable and noticeable only if he strained to read their messages of hope, appeared in muted colors as they dangled limply from flimsy, short poles that struggled to proclaim his pride, his strength, Lucy, their future together, their children, and his success.

While sprawled on the old wooden chair, he dreamed he was filling a bucket with water, and the appeal of another chance further quelled his restlessness and he sensed a calmness he could not recall ever experiencing. Ogden Royal and Tom Grillo appeared in the cinema of his mind and beckoned him to follow where he now knew he wanted to return.

As if by divine intervention, his dreams revealed his unfulfilled past did not have to dictate his future. How he had lived and why he had lived in such turmoil up to this point, he realized, was over because he had been so wrong. Why should he allow his life to be a testimonial to failure? A better relationship with those he loved, his mind continued to meander as he slept, could be his if he would embrace another chance to succeed at being a loving father and husband. He would seize this opportunity and ask his family to grant him forgiveness for his selfish and blind behavior. From this time forward, he would not squander another day, another moment looking back. He knew he could, he must, finally forgive the one person he had held as an unforgivable hostage and become more welcoming and loving toward those who loved him. This time, he was making a promise to himself he would keep.

He continued to dream about Ogden's story and the unexpected revelation that had brought him sleepless nights and anguish. He knew he must continue to fight the demon that had tempted him to end his life and bring hardship to Lucy and his children. He also realized that if he were to lead an honest and honorable life, he was compelled to tell Tom Arthur what Ogden had told him concerning the deaths of Billy Merritt and Tucker Warren. He would heed Tom's advice even if that meant involving the authorities and forfeiting the money.

As he stirred and awakened, he turned his head toward the table and became alarmed. What had he done with the pistol? He looked at the ground all around the table but the pistol was gone. What happened to the bottle of capsules he had left sitting on the table? Only the empty whiskey bottle and the water bottle remained where he had left them. The items that confirmed his depravity were no longer in sight. Perhaps he hadn't been dreaming when Grillo seemed to have appeared standing close by where he was sleeping.

At that moment, he felt a cool breeze that wafted across the lake and over where he now sat. As he glanced downward, he noticed one shoe lying on his left side and another shoe on his right. He then felt a gentle, cooling wind on his bare feet. How or when he had removed his shoes and socks, he didn't know. He did know, however, that for the first time for longer than he could determine, he didn't feel confined or bound. He was free, unshackled by an epiphany that had brought a life-saving wave of freedom.

He knew he had to leave for home as soon as possible. He gathered his journal from underneath a rock where he had placed it before Tom Grillo appeared to interrupt his plan. He had to get home to Lucy and he had to make things right for her, their children and for himself.

Epilogue

When his telephone rang long before the alarm clock was set to wake him, Sheriff Johnson realized this Saturday morning would not begin as he had planned. Even with his deputy sheriff off duty and out of town, he had hoped to stay in bed an extra hour or so and enjoy a little extra sleep. When he finally managed to locate the phone, the emergency dispatcher sounded uncharacteristically cheerful to awaken him and report a single vehicle accident that indicated possible bodily injury. Since he was the only officer available, necessity truncated the Sheriff's anticipated leisurely morning of rest. According to the initial report, a driver had lost control of a pick-up truck north of Grand Marais on Highway 61, about a mile beyond Five-Mile Rock. By the time he concluded the investigation and completed the official report back at his office, it was almost eleven o'clock and he was already tired and late for the planned morning drive of the Trail.

"Wilma, I'm finally making my daily drive up the Trail. I need to stop at Mayhew Lake on the way up and check on a fellow from Indiana who, according to a call I received yesterday, has been staying up there. Mrs. Tyler, his wife, called and was worried because she hadn't heard from him for a few days. Probably take me a little longer to make the trip today but I'll check in with you after I stop at Mayhew and again when I get up to Seagull and begin the drive back. Let me know if there's anything else that needs my attention while I'm on the road."

"Ya, sure. Be right here, Gus," Wilma Manygoats replied not looking up and without diverting her attention from whatever was on her computer screen that commanded her undivided attention. "Say, Gus," she said as she finally looked up at him and away from whatever had fascinated her a few seconds ago. "Gus," she continued her thought, "a fellow stopped here a few minutes ago asking for directions to Mayhew. Said he was from Indiana on the way to find his dad. If you see a fellow lookin' lost, it's probably him."

"Mrs. Tyler was worried when she called here yesterday. She must have called their son after she spoke with me and he decided to drive up here himself. Well, I'm on my way and I'll keep in touch, Wilma," Sheriff Johnson replied before he closed the door.

As he crested a hill, almost twenty miles up the Trail and only a few miles from his planned stop to check on Mr. Tyler, he noticed smoke before he saw a jack-knifed truck in the middle of the road. What been a load of pulpwood was now scattered on the pavement with several logs coming to rest in both side ditches. He pulled the cruiser off the road and grabbed a fire extinguisher. Joseph Two Bears, the truck driver, seemed fixated as he stood and stared at a car that had come to rest in a deep ditch on the same side of the road where the cruiser now sat.

"What happened here, Joe?" he asked the truck driver as he walked by the spellbound man and hurried toward the source of the smoke.

"Sheriff, that car came flyin' down the hill on the wrong side of the road," Joseph replied, as he pointed toward the wrecked car, "and headed right for me. I hit the brakes and tried to stop, tried to avoid hittin' it but the rear brakes let loose and the trailer jack-knifed. By the time the driver saw me and tried to get back over outta my way, it was too late. The skidding trailer and truck, pretty much formin' a flying vee, didn't allow much time for him or me to do much of anything," Joe answered, relieved by relating how the accident occurred, began to pace as he wiped sweat from his face and brow.

After he extinguished the small grass and pine needle fire that was beginning to spread, Sheriff Johnson noticed the Indiana license plate that was in plain view as the rear bumper of the car pointed skyward. The car was resting nose down in the ditch with the top smashed and mangled by colliding with the oncoming skidding trailer. Inside the car were what he supposed at first glance to be two men and one woman. The two men in the front-seat were unconscious and motionless as their shoulder harnesses held them upright. The front air bags had deployed and cascaded down the steering wheel and passenger-side dashboard like the airless balloons they had become. The driver's forehead had sustained a deep laceration just above eye-level and was bleeding profusely.

The male occupant on the passenger side sat slumped and leaning on the side door but did not display any observable outward injury. The woman passenger in the rear seat was conscious and moaning, trying to gain an upright position as she struggled to free herself from her seat restraint but in her dazed and confused state, couldn't seem to locate the latch that would release her. Sheriff Johnson helped her free herself and asked her name.

"I'm...Lucinda... Lucinda Tyler...what happened...where are my brothers...are they okay?"

"You just take it easy and I'll help you. My name is Gus Johnson, Sheriff Johnson. I'll get an ambulance up here just as fast as possible. The driver sustained a deep gash to his head. I don't know if he has any broken bones or other less obvious injuries. The man in the passenger seat is unconscious and I can't say to what extent he may be injured. As for you, do you think you can move and climb out of the car if I help you? Can you wiggle your toes and move your hands?" the sheriff offered.

"I think... I'm okay, just shook up and bruised," replied Lucinda. "I'm a doctor... so...if you will...if you can... get me out of here and on my feet...I need to do whatever I can to help...my brothers, Danny and John," she offered as she wiped away her tears and began to assume the purposeful role of a physician.

"Joe," the sheriff called out, again jolting the truck driver out of whatever daze he was experiencing, stopped pacing and turned toward the voice calling his name, "hurry and go to my car and get the emergency medical kit from the backseat and bring it to this lady. She needs to attend to the driver and get his bleeding stopped or slowed until the ambulance can get up here."

As Lucinda worked to help her brothers, the sheriff returned to the patrol car and called the station. "Wilma, I need ya to get a wrecker and an ambulance headed up here about seven miles north of the Brule River Bridge. I'm at a one-car and pulpwood truck accident scene. I have three people injured and one was bleeding badly from a deep cut to his forehead. After you call for the ambulance and wrecker, I need you to run Indiana license plate number 79-31461. The car is a 2001 or 2002, tan-colored, Ford Taurus. Get 'em movin' toward me and then get right back to me as soon as you can with information on the vehicle registration."

Within a few minutes, and long before he heard the approaching sirens heading to his location, Wilma called. "Gus, that plate and vehicle is registered to Daniel Tyler, Jr., West Lafayette, Indiana. I have rescue teams headed your way. Anything else you need?"

"No. There isn't much more I can do until I get some help…but let the rescue drivers know to hurry as much as possible," he answered.

Daniel and John Tyler's injuries were potentially crippling if not life threatening and neither awakened or responded to the emergency treatment administered by the ambulance staff. The injuries of both men were determined to warrant the medical services and technology available in a larger hospital that specialized in head and spinal cord injuries. The severity of their condition necessitated both men be airlifted from Grand Marais to a hospital in Duluth. Lucinda, who had escaped with bruises and a headache, was treated and admitted for observation at the Grand Marais Clinic.

As Sheriff Johnson watched as the second wrecker left the scene with Joe's truck in tow, he remembered the woman who had called him yesterday. He had almost promised her a positive outcome and relief from her anxiety. He had given her reason to expect him to call her back with good news but he now knew that call was going to be difficult to make.

Mrs. Tyler was staying close to her phone, he imagined, anxiously waiting for that call confirming all was well with her husband and her children had arrived safely. He had made many calls that brought news of death and injury, both by phone and in person throughout his career as a police officer. Experience and time had not made that duty easier.

"Wilma, we have this scene pretty well cleaned up and everything in place. I'm headed on up the Trail to inform Mr. Tyler concerning the whereabouts of his children, best as I can, and let him know his wife called me yesterday and has been worried about him. I'm sure he'll want to speak with his wife after I tell him what happened here. I don't know what to expect from Mr. Tyler and I can only speculate what may be going on between husband and wife but I think he is the person to contact her. They need to talk and then decide how they will proceed with this matter. I'll check back in with you when I'm finished at Mayhew Lake."

The End